———————— ★ ————————

"Mr. Samson? Mr. Pincus asked me to see to it that you got to your car. To escort you if necessary."

I looked up at him. He had black hair, black eyes and very white skin, the kind that looks good in bruises. "No thanks," I told him. "We can make it all right on our own."

I considered grabbing Rosie's arm and running like hell for the car. I couldn't bring myself to do it. A man has to try, at least, to keep his dignity, and besides, I wasn't all that sure Rosie would agree to run with me.

We walked very quickly to the car, got in and drove out of the lot.

"You know," Rosie said, "now that I think of it, Pincus wouldn't have people beaten up in his own parking lot. It would be bad for business. Can you imagine what the customers would think if they saw people getting beaten up right outside?"

"Yes. Which makes me wonder just exactly where he does plan on doing it."

———————— ★ ————————

A Forthcoming Worldwide Mystery by
SHELLEY SINGER

SPIT IN THE OCEAN

Pauline Straesser

FULL House

Shelley Singer

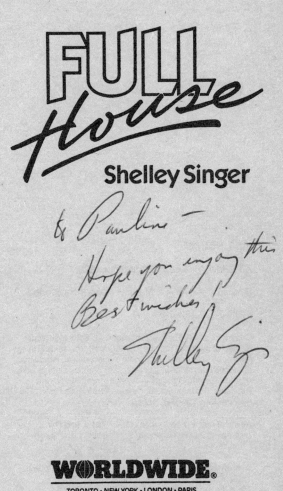

& Pauline —
Hope you enjoy this —
Best wishes,
Shelley S

W✺RLDWIDE.

TORONTO · NEW YORK · LONDON · PARIS
AMSTERDAM · STOCKHOLM · HAMBURG
ATHENS · MILAN · TOKYO · SYDNEY

FULL HOUSE

A Worldwide Mystery/September 1988

First published by St. Martin's Press Incorporated.

ISBN 0-373-26007-5

for Paula Solomon

The author thanks Inspector
Michel de Latour of the Berkeley
Police Department
and Tony Plotkin of Grainaissance,
Inc., for their help.

ONE

IF I HALF-CLOSED my eyes, I could pretend it was a movie set.

These were Vikings swarming all over the hull of a ship they were building so they could loot England or discover America before Columbus got there. The dark-haired guy was Tony Curtis; the blond was Kirk Douglas.

But I couldn't maintain the illusion. I had to open my eyes or risk tripping over the strewn building materials. This was the semivacant lot on the corner of my block, and I was there on a mission I could have lived without. I had to tell the Vikings they were making too much noise.

This particular lot had been the site of disputes for years. Zoning hassles. Permit fights. The owner kept trying to sell it—once to a fast-food chain, once to a less-than-reputable church—and the neighbors, who wanted nothing but low-density, high-priced housing, kept stopping him. Now the owner, in a fit of despair and possibly in the spirit of revenge, had rented it to some people for what was supposed to be a temporary building project.

Back in foggy July, when they'd started, my neighbor Rico had asked them what they were working on. "A ship," they'd told him. But nobody believed that. Rico, a seventy-six-year-old patriarch who spoke just enough English to pick up and relay slightly skewed local news, must have gotten it wrong. A ship. Several miles from San Francisco Bay, in the middle of the North Oakland flatlands. Now, in hot September, they were far enough along so you could see he hadn't gotten it wrong. It was a ship.

At least 150 feet long and 40 feet wide. On a vacant city lot. Lately, they'd been working longer hours seven days a week, speeding the project along.

That was the problem, and that was why I was there. Rico again. The old man lived right next to the lot. And, he told me piteously, they were keeping him awake with their hammering, sawing, and, worst of all, cheerful singing, from about six in the morning until ten or so at night. Rico liked to take naps, and he liked to go to bed with the sun.

I told him they were close enough to legal noisemaking hours so we wouldn't get much help from the law. I suggested Rico might want to talk to the Vikings and ask them to be quiet in the evening.

The corners of his mouth drooped depressively. "Come on, Jake," he said. "You think they gonna listen to an old man?" He shook his head sadly, watching me out of the corners of his eyes. "You talk to them. You the tough guy on the block."

Which didn't say much for the block. But Rico's a good neighbor. He has fed my cats and kept an eye on my house a number of times when I had to be away.

So there I was, down at the once-vacant lot, trying to look friendly but firm, approaching the ship. More than a dozen sweating, sunburned workers were crawling around on the scaffolding. I hailed the nearest one and he jumped to the ground from a plank about five feet up. Like a cat. Better than my cats, who are getting soft with age.

He was a young man, shirtless, muscular, with light brown hair and eyes the color of the blue in my blue and white 1953 Chevy Bel Air.

"Yes sir? What can I do for you?"

I don't like being called sir. I'm only thirty-nine.

"Nice looking ship you've got there. Big."

had belonged to Beatrice's meditation group and a few other groups as well.

"Yes, sure. Nice to see you again. How's the meditation center doing?"

She shrugged. "I don't know. I'm into a more integrated life-style now."

"Oh, good."

"You're a writer, aren't you?"

"In a way." In no way. I had credentials from *Probe Magazine*, a San Francisco investigative monthly, but I'd gotten them from a pal, one of the editors. It was a trade off. I needed to cover my tail when I was running around doing things I had no business doing, like tracking killers. My friend figured he might get a story out of me once in a while. I need some kind of paper; I don't have P.I. credentials. I don't even have a license to catch fish.

"Are you here to find out about Noah?"

Wolfe, who'd been measuring one of the boards he'd been fiddling with, looked up. "Excuse me, Beatrice," he said. "Could you help me with this?"

It sounded like an order, and she responded as if it were.

"I must go now, Jake," she said sweetly. "I hope I see you again."

Walking home, I wondered briefly how much more time my little good-neighbor chore was going to take. Briefly, because I had other things on my mind. In a couple of hours, the peace and privacy of my home was going to be lovingly shattered by the arrival, for a visit, of my father and stepmother. She had a niece in the Bay Area; he had me. They had decided to take a vacation and "kill two birds with one stone." They would be staying with me. And since my house has no spare bedroom, I had given them mine. I would sleep on the sofa bed in the living room. The sofa an ex-girlfriend, back when it had been my only bed, had called "the steel trap."

My father had been sketchy about the length of their stay. I was meeting their six o'clock plane at Oakland International.

I walked up my driveway, past the vegetable garden that my tenant, Rosie Vicente, and I struggled sporadically to maintain. The tomatoes needed watering. Rosie, whose cottage is tucked behind some trees just back of the garden, wasn't home from work yet. Too bad. It would have been nice to have a beer together.

Tigris and Euphrates, in the way of cats, heard me coming and demanded food. I met their demands, pulled a beer from the refrigerator, and settled back with an Ellery Queen I'd read three times before, front door open, hot sun painting a bent yellow rectangle on floor and wall.

I hadn't read more than a chapter when I heard someone coming up my front steps. A tentative rap on the doorframe.

"Mr. Samson?" It was Arnold Wolfe. "I'm sorry to disturb you . . ."

"You want to talk about the noise problem?"

"Not exactly. Beatrice tells me you do investigative reporting or something like that."

"Would you like a beer?"

"No, thanks. Beatrice says you might be able to help us."

"Look, Arnold, I'm not exactly a reporter."

"Beatrice says some friends of hers were very impressed with some work you did once. Something about a murder you investigated."

"I didn't write a story about the murder."

"Exactly," he said. "She says she heard you solved it. Could you solve something for us?"

"I'm not a detective."

"Well, then, what are you?" His voice went up an octave. This man was not in good shape. I ignored the question, because I never know how to answer it.

"What is it you want, Arnold?"

"Would you work for us if we paid you?"

"I don't even know who 'us' is, for Christ's sake." I was getting irritated, but the part about paying me was filtering through the irritation.

"Do you have a glass of wine?" he asked. I brought him a glass of California red. The man was so shaky I was afraid he'd drop one of my good supermarket wineglasses and stain my garage-sale rug. He took a healthy slug before he spoke.

"It's about Noah."

"I've heard that name before."

"Noah is our leader. Our spiritual leader and our leader in the work we're doing." He hesitated. "He's disappeared and the police won't help because they say he went off on his own. But we know he wouldn't. We know something terrible has happened, and we need him."

"For this work you're doing? Something to do with building that ship?"

"Yes, and I suppose that's the first thing you have to know. It's not just a ship."

TWO

THE BEL AIR skimmed south along 580, its rebuilt engine humming, its driver mumbling to himself.

I'd accepted Arnold Wolfe's advance of $500 on the offer of $150 a day plus expenses. I'd also accepted the stipulation that if he wasn't satisfied with my progress in a week the arrangement would terminate. If he was more than satisfied, on the other hand, the per diem would go up to $200. We'd also reached a tentative agreement on that other matter: He would see if he could get more people to work during the day so they could stop a little earlier; I would see if that arrangement would be acceptable to "my people."

The plane from Chicago was late. I had half an hour to spare. The plastic seats at gate 15 didn't look inviting but I sat down anyway.

Wolfe had hesitated a bit at my demand for an advance, but I had refused to start without it once I'd heard his story.

This group, with Noah as its organizer and leader, believed that a series of tidal waves was about to inundate the world, drowning all the continents. The first wave, Arnold said, was due to start swallowing North America by January 1, which meant that they had only a little more than three months to finish their arks. That's arks, plural. They had two: the one on my corner and another up in Sonoma County near the Russian River. The people who worked on the arks, and their families, would be the only ones saved when the world went under.

So they really believed, as the muscular young ark-builder had told me, that when the vessels were finished, they would be "afloat." Arnold had cut that conversation short because they didn't want people outside the group knowing about the project. It was like the old story about the fallout shelter. Once it started raining, everyone would try to get in.

But a problem had come up. Noah had disappeared. He had left a note for his wife and he had gone away, apparently with a woman and certainly with a quarter of a million dollars of his own money that he had promised to invest in the arks.

Arnold was afraid that he wouldn't be able to finish the arks without the money, but even if they could somehow make up for the loss, he said, they could not make up for the loss of their leader. The police wouldn't help because the note was in Noah's handwriting and he hadn't taken anyone's money but his own. They said it looked like the man had simply run off with a woman. Arnold said that there were even some rumors among the ark group itself that Noah had abandoned them. But that was impossible. He would never have run off. He would never have lost faith and he would never have left his wife. Arnold was sure that Noah had been kidnapped, at the very least.

Like the police, I had my doubts. Unlike the police, I had time and nothing much to do. Also unlike the police, I stood to make some money on the deal, and my own funds were getting a little low.

I don't mind working for crazies, as long as they're not bad crazies. These people seemed to be reasonably okay crazies. They weren't blaming the flood on any particular group of people or any particular life-style or set of beliefs. They included in their number all kinds of people, as

long as said people, according to Arnold, led "lives of love
and peace."

What they were blaming it on, as it turned out, was what
Arnold called "mankind's violation of our covenant with
God." It wasn't so much that people were doing a lot of
bad things, he explained, it was that we weren't following
God's law by punishing the wicked. An eye for an eye. A
life for a life.

"All legal?" I asked suspiciously.

"All very legal," he hastened to assure me. They believed in the law, and that the law should be used to pun-
ish and protect. To kill the killers and stop the
victimization of the innocent.

I reflected that Noah's bunch were, so to speak, riding
a wave. Killing the killers. I remembered reading about a
national poll that showed a clear thirty-year cycle. In 1953,
nearly seventy percent of the population favored the death
penalty. By 1966 that figure had crashed to around forty
percent. By 1985 it was up in the seventies again, and if I
remember correctly, was the highest it had been since polls
were taken. There was nothing simple about the reason, or
at least I didn't think so. It wasn't just because people were
returning to fifties-style conservatism, although there was
some of that in it. It wasn't just because history moves in
thirty-year cycles, although it sure seems to. No, what
happened was closer to this: life itself changed. Cities
changed. In the forties and early fifties retribution was
simply an ethical and philosophical issue. Most people
weren't exposed to that much crime or that many criminals. When legal fashion began to change, about the time
we started trying to understand everybody, no one worried too much. The same people who had gone along with
the old eye for an eye, that same mass of Americans who
hadn't been exposed to much crime, went along with the

mood. They were, after all, civilized people, and believed in keeping up with the times.

By the end of the sixties, though, a new element had come into it. Nearly everyone, at least those who lived in or near a city of any size, now had the opportunity to learn about crime and criminals firsthand. Suddenly, or so it seemed, there was a huge criminal class of people who thought being pissed off generally was a good excuse. Crime was no longer academic and the criminal was not someone you never had to meet, a poor oppressed product of an unjust or unfeeling or economically tilted society. He was the son of a bitch with the lead pipe in his hand who'd strolled up to you on the street, the one who'd paid for your skull fracture with less than a year in prison. And now everybody was pissed off. Killing the killers. Right, Noah, I thought. That's the wave of the future.

The figures from that national poll—Gallup, it was—had stuck with me for strong personal reasons. That low point for retribution, 1966? That was the year I became a cop, back in Chicago. The summer of love hadn't happened yet, and the summer of hate was still two years off. I was a pretty idealistic kid. I wanted to be a cop to protect good people. Chicago was a hard town, people barricaded inside their neighborhoods, spitting over the line into the alien territory next door. But I believed everything was going to get better. We were beginning to understand people, see, beginning to understand why criminals were criminals. If we understood, we could maybe make it all better. And I was going to help. Sixty-six was okay.

Sixty-seven was not bad, although, as a cop, I wished the hippies would wave their dope around a little less. Then came 1968, summer, the Democratic Convention. Chicago in the summer is bad enough without the smell of tear

gas. Somehow, in the middle of the mess, I stopped a kid
who was coming at me, a long-haired kid waving a sign
that said "Make Love Not War." I stopped him with my
truncheon, and I saw the blood pour down his face, and I
saw his friend carry him off. That was pretty much it for
me. That whole, bloody, stinking time, with kids rioting
and the "leaders" who didn't give a shit how many of
them got hurt. The leaders who knew the Chicago cops
were rotten and would be encouraged to be rotten and bust
heads and lob tear gas canisters into the yards of citizens,
and generally prove they were the pigs these people said
they were. That whole bloody stinking time. I was a scared
kid and I just knew that the kid I'd hit had been an innocent, an idealist, a peace-lover pushed to the edge of stu-
pidity. I didn't report for roll call the next morning. I never
went back to the force. I lit out for California, the northern part, and wandered around doing odd jobs, soaking up
the culture, helping out a few friends who got in trouble,
living on a commune, living with a woman, getting married and getting divorced and moving, eventually, to the
metropolitan East Bay, to Berkeley and then across the
border to Oakland. I was a Chicago boy, a city kid, returned to his roots. And I could understand how other city
kids might want to believe God was going to wash away all
the bad guys, the ones who made innocent people bleed.

So even though Arnold was clearly nuts, I had decided
to take his money.

Flight 501 from Chicago was coming in for a landing.

I got up and stood near the ramp entrance as the passengers began emerging, swarming with relief from their
portable environment to solid, stationary airport. Although I was looking hard, I didn't see my parents until
they were nearly on me. They're both short, and a little
plump. It was my father's shirt I saw first, a red and blue

Hawaiian number. This was not a concession to current fashion, but a decades-old concession to alien places. He'd been to visit me only a couple of times since I'd moved west; his ideas of California remained unshakably L.A., and his idea of L.A. came, I think, from Alan Ladd movies.

Eva was wearing a turquoise polyester pants suit. She grabbed me before my father had a chance to, and damned near squeezed the life out of me, planting a lipstick kiss on my lips. Then it was his turn. He hugged me close for a few seconds, then, pushing me away with his hands on my biceps, looked me up and down.

"So, bum? How are you?"

"Isaac!" Eva laughed. "Is that something to call your only son? Such a doll, too."

"A doll in blue jeans." He shook his head, but he was smiling.

Eva patted my stomach. "A little more weight, maybe, since I saw you last?"

I shrugged. "I'm on a diet," I lied.

It took a while to get their luggage, not because the service was slow, but because there was so much of it. Two big ones, three medium, and two canvas bags. I took the two big ones and a bag. My father picked up the three medium ones, grunted, and handed one to Eva.

When we got to the Chevy he looked at it the way he'd looked at me. I braced myself, but he surprised me.

"Hah! Now, that's what a car should look like. Like an automobile."

That was great, but, it turned out, he also believed a house should look like a house and a yard should look like a yard.

"What is this?" he wanted to know, as we trudged up the gravel driveway. "A farm?"

"That's the vegetable garden, Pa."

"In the front yard?"

"In this neighborhood," I told him, "you show off your vegetables."

We passed Rosie's cottage.

"This is where the Italian lives?" They knew Rosie's name and they knew she was my friend. Like most of the immigrant generation, they approved of Italians, even if they *were* Catholic.

I nodded. "That's the cottage."

"Could use a little paint," Eva said. The cedar shingles were only five years old. I wondered what they'd say about the house. I'd started painting the exterior stucco three years before, and, tiny as the place is, I'd never quite managed to find the time to finish. It's half pale pink and half white. The trim is half scabrous white and half dark green. They didn't say anything, which is, for them, the ultimate comment.

We dumped the bags in the middle of the living room.

"This," I pointed to the steel trap, "is a sofa bed, where I will sleep. You get the bedroom."

"We wouldn't think of it," Eva said quickly, before my father got his mouth open. "We wouldn't want to put you out."

"Eva," I kissed her on the cheek. "You couldn't possibly do that."

THREE

THEY GOT UP at seven the next morning, tiptoeing heavily around the house until I crawled out of the trap.

"I'll bet you always get up this early, right?" I asked, untwisting my pajama bottoms—I don't normally wear anything to bed—and accepting a cup of coffee.

"Sure," my father replied. "If you had a job you'd get up early, too."

"I have a job," I grumped. "I just hadn't planned on starting it before nine or so."

Eva made oatmeal. I had a piece of toast, showered, dressed, wandered around the yard for a while, and got underway by nine-thirty.

Following the directions Arnold had given me, I took Claremont Avenue into Berkeley and turned up Ashby, passing the Claremont Hotel. Actually, they call it a resort hotel, but I can never quite get myself to accept the idea of a resort in Berkeley. The massive turn-of-the-century structure occupies acres of insanely expensive real estate. It straddles the Berkeley/Oakland line, but for some reason the management says it's in Oakland. Must have something to do with taxes. Nothing else that is able to say it's in Berkeley ever says it's in Oakland.

I took the second left after the hotel and started the uphill climb through some other very expensive real estate. When I found the house, my first thought was that if all this belonged to me I'd drown before I'd trade it in on a crowded ark.

It had a circular driveway, something you don't see very often outside of old movies. The middle of the bagel was a mass of flowers and shrubs. The grounds looked big enough and complicated enough to require a full-time gardener. The house itself was one of those Georgian neo-classic numbers with the Greek columns across the front.

One car was parked in the driveway. It was a big, new, expensive American car. I don't know what kind. All big, new, expensive cars look alike to me. I pulled up behind it. The steps leading up to the portico were wide, and so was the portico. The front door had a fanlight. The bell was a three-note chime.

A thirtyish maid with a sullen freckled face and bright orange hair answered the door. At least I guessed she was a maid. She was wearing a droopy shirtwaist dress and white tennis shoes instead of a cute little uniform, but she was carrying an open bottle of furniture polish. She was a flaw in the fantasyland of this house, and I was still resenting that when she told me Mrs. Gerhart would see me in the den. Georgian houses don't have dens.

Still clutching her bottle, she led me across a large entry hall with—sure enough—a wide stairway curving down from a gallery, and ushered me through a large door. She didn't announce me, she just turned and padded away.

The den was a dim hideaway that had been designed as a library. An easy deduction: the walls were lined with shelves. The woman who rose from the brown leather couch to greet me was in her late forties. She was wearing a full skirt that came halfway down her calves, high-heeled pumps, and a short-sleeved blouse with a Peter Pan collar and a ruffle down the front. Her blond hair was styled in a slightly updated bastard version of the Italian Boy cut of the fifties. She had an upturned nose, red lipstick, and a bright smile.

"Mr. Samson," she said pertly, "I'm so happy to meet you. Arnold has told me so much about you." Arnold didn't know so much about me, and it was probably just as well, but I nodded agreeably and took a seat in the matching leather chair she offered me. "Adele is bringing sherry. I hope you like sherry?"

I assumed Adele was the maid who had let me in. I hoped she would put down the furniture polish before she poured the drinks. I said that sherry would be fine.

"You'll have to ask me questions—may I call you Jake?—because I really don't know what you need to know. Call me June."

"Well, June, for a start, why don't you just tell me a little bit about your husband. Your history together, his interests, his friends, that kind of thing."

"Should I start way back at the beginning?"

"Sure." I wanted to get a picture of the man who had married this fifties princess and become first a rich man and then a cult leader. And I wanted to get a feel for his wife.

"Okay. Let's see, we met in 1957, at college. He was in graduate school. I was a junior, in education. We met at a sorority party. He was going to be a chemist. I thought that was wonderful." Yeah, I thought. In 1957 everyone wanted to be a chemist or an engineer and have a great job forever. My mother, may she rest in peace, had wanted me to be a nuclear physicist when I grew up.

She continued. "I admired him so much. All my friends envied me." She sighed.

"By the way," I interjected, "is his real name Noah?"

"Oh, good heavens no. His real name is Thomas. Anyway, we were married just two weeks after he got his master's. I decided I really didn't need a degree, myself. Of course, he got a job immediately. We bought our first lit-

tle house. That was back in Ohio. Cleveland. We settled
down to raise a family." She sighed again. "But we didn't
have one." So much for her generation's American Dream.
"They thought it was because he'd had mumps. Well,
things just sort of went along like that. We lived in Cleveland, then Texas. He had wonderful jobs and life was very
good. We saved lots of money. But in 1968 or there-
abouts, Thomas began to be unhappy. He began to have
nightmares. He began to talk about...well, he said he was
contributing to the poisoning of the planet. One day he
just sat me down and he said, June, I want to move to
California and open a health food business. Well, you can
just about imagine.... But he said he'd worked all those
years and made all that money, and he thought there was
even more he could make in health food. He said health
food and vitamins and things were going to get very big.
And you know, Jake, he'd always been right. After all, I
had to give him credit for that. He always knew about
trends, that's why he became a chemist in the first place.
So I said, okay, Thomas, I guess you know what you're
talking about."

We were interrupted by the arrival of Adele with the
sherry. Two glasses and a bottle on a tray, no furniture
polish.

"Thank you, Adele," she said. Adele left without answering. "So to make a long story short, we moved here.
First thing, he opened a store, to get the feel of the business. Then, sure enough, he began to expand. Before I
knew it, he was wholesaling and then he had farms and
brand names and everything. That was all in five or six
years, I forget which."

This guy, I thought, was a real whiz. I began to wonder
how he figured to make money out of arks.

"And then what happened?" I prompted.

"We got rich." She smiled and sipped her sherry. "But that wasn't enough for Thomas. He is a seeker. He began to study religion. Oh, not just Christianity, you know, but all kinds of things. And then, just a couple of years ago, he started having dreams again. Nightmares. And then he starting getting messages about a flood. That was when he took the name Noah and started organizing these arks. Well, I hate to admit it, Jake, but I thought he was crazy. I begged him to go see a therapist. He wouldn't and he wouldn't and then he finally did, somebody here in Berkeley, and he came home and said the therapist told him he was okay and if he wanted to organize arks he certainly had the money and the time and why shouldn't he? I don't know if the therapist actually said that, but what could I do? He seemed all right otherwise. I certainly didn't believe there was going to be a flood, but he was happy, and I thought, what if it's true? I'd certainly want to be on the ark."

"What happened to the health food business? Did he sell it?"

"Oh, no. Yellow Brick Farms is still going strong. Although it hasn't been easy with Thomas concentrating on the arks."

"You've been running the business, then?"

"Oh, no. There's his partner Joe, Joe Durell. He's running things. I admire him tremendously, but I'm sure it's difficult, not having Thomas. He's understaffed right now, too, besides that. And of course he's been helping with the arks all along.... Jake, Thomas would never leave me. He's been kidnapped, or maybe he's been murdered." Her eyes filled with moisture. Her hand shook and she set down her sherry glass and poured it half full again. I accepted another one. She looked up at me and the tears spilled over. "I hope you can help us."

"I hope I can, too. So, this Durell's running Noah's business affairs, and he's involved in the arks?'' She nodded. "And Arnold's running Noah's ark affairs? Is he also involved in the business?''

"No." She placed her sherry glass on a side table without taking a sip.

"Why keep the business going, I mean, if you believe there's going to be a flood?''

"Oh, Jake, you can't just put people out of work. Joe was very concerned about that. And then it brings in money, of course. Along with the casino."

"The casino?''

"We have a casino up at Tahoe. Well, a part interest in one."

Of course, I thought. I asked her if there were any other major business interests I should know about, and she said there weren't. That was a relief.

There were a lot of things I needed to know about Noah neé Thomas Gerhart, but the most important item, at the moment, was the one that came last in the scheme of things: the dear June letter he'd left his wife before he'd disappeared. I asked to see it. She nodded, businesslike, and handed me a file folder that had been lying on one of the bookshelves.

I opened it. It contained an original and two photocopies of the letter. I took out the original. It was six days old, dated September 14.

My Dear June:

I have gone to do something I have to do. I can't tell you how long it will take or even if I will be back at all. I can't tell you what I'm doing or why because it's better for you not to know, and the last thing I want is to see you get hurt. But I have to do this. Tell Arnold for me, please, and tell him that Marjorie is with me.

Love,
Noah

The note was handwritten.

"What do you think about this?" I asked carefully.

"I think it was written under duress by someone who wanted the money."

"You don't think he's just run away with this Marjorie—what's her last name?—to have an affair or something?"

"Of course not. Her name is Burns."

"You know her, then?"

"We've met. She's a loyal worker. That's really all I know about her, except that she's black."

"Can you describe her?"

"Not really."

"I'd like to have this," I said, waving the note.

"You may have one of the copies," she said softly. I went along with her. She wanted the original, she could have it. I stuck the original back in the folder and kept one of the copies.

She'd found the note, she said, propped up on her dining room table that afternoon when she'd come home from shopping. She'd taken it to Arnold. The two of them had agonized for a couple of days, finally deciding to take the note to the police. The original. The police hadn't wanted it. They'd asked two questions: "Is this his handwriting?" and "Does the missing money belong to him?" Yes it was and yes it did, so that was that.

Arnold had known how much money was involved, because it was the amount he and Noah had decided was necessary to cover the remaining construction of the arks,

and for supplies, seeds, tools, and equipment for the new
world they were planning on building. As before, Noah
would hand over the money to Arnold, who would deposit it in the ark account and oversee its disbursement.
Mrs. Noah also knew how much was to be handed over,
and knew that the check her husband had written—with no
payee listed in the check register—had nearly depleted the
account from which ark money was usually taken. The
check had been dated, according to the register, September 14, the day he had disappeared.

"Do you normally keep that kind of money in a checking account?" The question was half investigation, half
awe.

"Certainly not," she said. "It had to be put there on
purpose."

I should hope so. "Couldn't he just transfer the funds
somehow?"

"He enjoyed handing it over personally. He and Arnold liked to make a little ceremony out of it." Did I catch
a slightly patronizing touch there? Probably not.

I asked her if she could put together a list of people who
were close to Noah before I left her that day. She said there
weren't very many. His partner at Yellow Brick Farms, his
partner in Tahoe, and a few others. No relatives.

"Another thing," I said. "His car. I saw one parked in
the drive."

"Oh, that's mine. They must have kidnapped him in his
car."

It was a blue 1975 Volvo station wagon, "kind of beat
up." I guess I must have raised an eyebrow, because she
went on to explain. "He was very attached to it. He was
always having it worked on. He said it suited him and he
saw no reason to get a new one."

"And the car is missing."

"Yes. I suppose if the police found it blown up or something they'd take the trouble to look for him." She sounded bitter. I asked for the license number, and wrote it in my pocket notebook along with her description of the car.

"Does he have a study or an office here at home? Some kind of room he uses for his own stuff?"

She nodded.

"I'd like to have a look around, see if I can find anything that might give me a lead."

"Upstairs," she said reluctantly. "Second door on the left. Please, try not to disturb anything."

"I may need to take some of it home with me."

She sighed a poor, ragged little sigh.

"And while I'm up there, maybe you could make out that list of his friends." She agreed that maybe she could.

I had never in my life walked up a staircase like that one, not even in a museum. I felt like Cary Grant, or maybe George Washington.

Noah's office was plain and sparsely furnished. A leather couch, like the one downstairs, a recliner, a desk and swivel chair, two four-drawer file cabinets. Nothing on the desk. The bookshelves were heavy on philosophy and religion, with nutrition and farming running a poor second. There were no chemistry books that I could see. The desk was locked, but the file cabinets weren't.

They contained a lot of the usual debris, mostly personal financial records, old tax forms, and correspondence. Way in the back of the bottom drawer I found his old master's thesis, which seemed to have something to do with oil refining, I say seemed because H_2O is about all I have managed to retain from high school chemistry and my brain goes dyslexic—or is it aphasic?—the second it realizes it is being asked to read something technological.

The financial files told me only what I already knew: the man was rich and he was building arks. There were a couple of slim folders about the health food business and the casino, but it looked like most of the business files were stashed at the businesses themselves.

I pulled about a dozen file folders and stacked them on the desk to take with me. They included the names of people involved in working on the two arks, a couple hundred names, and some personal papers.

June peeked diffidently in the door. "I'm finished," she said, waving a green steno pad.

"Great. These lists of ark-workers, are they complete?"

"I don't think so. Arnold would know."

"The desk is locked," I informed her. "Do you have a key?"

"I don't know. I could look for one." She didn't want to.

"I don't want to force the lock, but . . ."

"Oh, please don't. He was very attached to that desk."

I reflected grumpily that it was too bad the man was more attached to his possessions than he was to his sanity. She handed me the steno pad and went off to look for a key.

Meanwhile, I thumbed through the ark names. On the Oakland list, I recognized a couple of names. Arnold and Beatrice, and Marjorie Burns. I found Noah's Yellow Brick partner near the bottom of the Sonoma list.

I opened the steno pad. Durell was listed, and the casino partner, whose name was Jerry Pincus. Arnold. A guy named Bert Olson, who was, according to the scribble beside his name, Noah's auto mechanic. That was it. Pincus was apparently not involved in the arks, or at least his name wasn't on the lists I had.

June reappeared with a key. "I think this is it." I took it and tried it. The desk drawer slid open.

"Are Pincus and Olson in on the arks?" I asked her, pulling out two old checkbooks, a dog rabies certificate dated 1976, a few photos of June and a man who was probably Noah. Odds and ends.

"No, Jerry doesn't believe in them. I don't know Bert...I've met him once or twice."

I found an address book. "Is this current?" She looked through it.

"Not really," she answered. "It's from Houston."

"Do you have a more current one?"

"He must have it with him if it's not in the desk."

I pawed through the other drawers. A lot of ballpoint pens, paperclips, junk. I have seen neater desks, but not at my house.

"Is this Noah?" I asked, pointing to one of the snapshots.

"I have better pictures of him if you want one."

"I do."

We walked down the stairs together. She didn't remind me of either Katharine Hepburn or Martha Washington. And since I was carrying file folders, I couldn't have any illusions about myself.

"This list you gave me," I began. She looked attentive. "These are all the people who were closest to him?"

"Besides me," she chirped.

"Shouldn't Marjorie be on it?"

She reddened slightly. "Yes, well, I suppose...she has worked closely with him...." She took the list from me and added the name Marjorie Burns at the bottom. Then, angrily, "But certainly not as closely as the police seem to think."

"Anyone else you might have forgotten?" I tried to sound kindly.

"No."

"If you think of anyone, give me a call." I ripped a corner off the mostly blank page listing Noah's closest buddies and wrote my number down for her.

Then I took the file folders and the photo of Noah she'd given me and drove down to the Berkeley Marina, where I sat on the grass reading, thinking, and watching people and dogs playing. When the sherry wore off, I had a couple of tacos at a place on University Avenue and headed for home.

FOUR

EVA WAS BROWNING a hunk of boneless chuck.

"Such a stove," she said. "I haven't seen a stove like this since World War II. The burner…fut-fut-fut." Tigris and Euphrates were entangling themselves in her legs, crazed by the smell of meat. "You should feed the cats."

I did as I was told. "It works okay," I said, defending my stove. "The other burners don't go fut-fut-fut."

"I always make pot roast on the front left. I'm too old to change."

"Where's Pa?"

"Taking a walk. He wants to see what all the noise is about down on the corner. I met your tenant today. She's coming for dinner." Eva's tone was even, unrevealing. I wondered what kind of costume Rosie had been wearing when they met. She has two favorite tee shirts. One is imprinted with the head of Gertrude Stein, the other, Marilyn Monroe.

The meat was brown. Eva added water, sliced onion, celery tops, and a bay leaf.

"She always drives a truck?"

"She's a carpenter. She needs it for work."

"Such a beautiful girl. It's a new world nowadays, that's for sure."

"Parts of it, anyway," I said. "How did you meet Rosie?" I sat on the stepstool to watch her cutting up potatoes and carrots.

"I was watering your tomatoes. She came home. I told her six-thirty. The dog is coming, too. A beautiful dog."

Rosie has a middle-aged black standard poodle named
Alice B. Toklas. Eva dropped the pieces of potato in salted
cold water and let them sit on top of the stove. The cut-up
carrots went in the refrigerator. "Tomorrow," she said,
"I'll defrost your refrigerator. And now I think I'll take a
nap." She wiped her hands on her apron. Actually, it was
my apron, a canvas one with "Berkeley Lumber Company" printed on the front. A present from Rosie. Eva
went into the bedroom. I walked down to the cottage.

Rosie's worked with me on two other cases, and I was
wondering if she might have some time to help out on this
one. At the very least, I needed to do some thinking out
loud.

Alice, dozing on the small front deck, opened her eyes,
waged her undocked tail, and got up to accompany me inside. Rosie offered me a beer.

The cottage is a big L-shaped room with a Franklin stove
in one corner. The small part of the ell is the kitchen. We
sat at the table and looked out the French windows at the
cottage yard, an enclosed, ivy-hung island of privacy.

"She's making pot roast," I said.

"Good. I'll pick up a bottle of burgundy and a bottle of
Mogen David. Think that will do it?"

"Manischewitz is okay, too."

Rosie was wearing a red tank top, cutoffs, and cowboy
boots. No Stein. No Monroe. There was a fine powder of
sawdust on her short dark hair.

"Got a case," I said casually.

"When do you need me? I'm finishing a garage conver-
sion this week."

"What are you converting it to?"

"A master bedroom."

"I need you whenever you can come in on it."

She laughed, and I knew why. On my first two cases I'd been reluctant, to say the least, to involve Rosie. For one thing, they included corpses. For another, they required dealing with some pretty unsavory types. Rosie's not exactly pink cotton candy, but she is my friend, and I guess I had been feeling protective. I still did, but I was determined not to show it because it really infuriated her. Also, I would never have tied those cases up so neatly if Rosie hadn't been around. We were a good team.

"Does this one pay anything?"

"Sure does. You can have fifty-fifty on the per diem any day you work." I gave her the financial picture.

"I'm free most of next week, and if we're still on it after that I can get out of the next job. Just a deck, and I'm helping a couple of friends. No rush, no problem." She sipped at her beer.

I told her who the clients were.

"Noah's ark," she said. "And vitamins. And a casino." She got us each another beer. "You know, I saw a piece on them in the *Chronicle* a couple of months ago."

"About the arks?" I found that hard to believe. The street would have been besieged by reporters and freaks.

"Not exactly. A reporter came around to check them out and they told her they were building a ship. That it was an educational project of some kind, that they hadn't been able to get space on the Bay, and that they were going to dismantle it when the project was over. Tiny little blurb. I guess the press kind of lost interest after that."

I showed her the wallet-sized photo June had given me. "It's a few years old," I said. "But she says he looks pretty much the same except his beard's a little longer." We both gazed at the picture. A pale dark-haired man. Fine-looking frizzy hair. Crisp short beard. Pale eyes—gray, she'd told me—that looked mildly bewildered. This was after the successful establishment of Yellow Brick Farms but long before the arks. I told Rosie I had a description and license number for his car, too.

She thought in silence for a while. "So maybe he's kidnapped and maybe he's dead and maybe he's in a motel room with Marjorie. What do you think?"

I shrugged, remembering the orange-haired Adele. "I think the maid did it."

FIVE

ROSIE ARRIVED for dinner promptly at six-thirty, Alice leading the way. She was dressed conservatively in white pants with drawstrings at waist and ankles, Birkenstock sandals, and a peach-colored silk blouse. I hoped she wouldn't spill any gravy; she was pretty dressed up.

Eva beamed, and offered her a glass of Mogen David. Rosie was not willing to go that far, and asked for burgundy.

The evening was cool, so I'd laid a tiny fire in the Franklin stove for coziness. Eva maneuvered things so that Rosie and I wound up on the couch.

"So," Eva said, "you're a carpenter. You make kitchen cabinets, that kind of thing I suppose?"

"Sure."

"She also builds houses," I added. What was this kitchen cabinet crap? Rosie tossed me a look that said she didn't need my help, but thanks for the thought.

"Jake could use some new cabinets. He should hire you." Of course—I knew she was thinking this—if I married Rosie I wouldn't have to pay. "All this carpentering," she continued, "it doesn't make your hands calloused?" I stayed out of it. Rosie smiled.

"A little," she admitted, "but I use a lot of hand cream." I glanced down at her hands. I'd never really noticed anything but their shape before. They looked smooth. Amazing.

Eva took a sip of her Mogen David. My father came out of the bedroom, pink from his shower, knotting a striped tie.

"Ah! I thought I heard voices. The carpenter's here." He could hardly have avoided hearing voices, since the house is about six hundred square feet. "Can I bring somebody a little wine?"

I asked for burgundy. He brought the bottle in from the kitchen.

"So tell me, Rosie," he said, settling in the rocker beside the fireplace. "I hear a lot of people in San Francisco don't eat meat."

Rosie hesitated. "Well, I have friends in San Francisco, and some of them—I suppose that's true...."

I turned to her, feeling that an explanation was needed. "He means the Bay Area. The City, Marin County, the East Bay, the Peninsula, maybe even Sonoma, Napa—they're all San Francisco."

"Oh, right, in that case, sure. There are a lot of people who don't eat it, or eat less of it, or don't eat red meat. But isn't that true in Chicago?"

"Who knows? Red meat. Huh. Red meat. Like pot roast." He turned to Eva. "See, I said you should ask. Maybe she don't eat pot roast."

"I eat pot roast," Rosie said quickly. I knew she didn't eat red meat often, but Rosie is not inflexible. As for me, there is no life without pot roast. Because I'm a man of the eighties, and because middle age threats are closing in, I don't eat pot roast every night.

Having exhausted that topic of conversation, my father went on to better ones.

"You're a carpenter," he said. "You should get a job with those crazy people on the corner. The ones who are building a boat." He was kidding. Rosie saw that, and laughed.

"I don't know much about shipbuilding," she said, "and I don't think they're hiring, anyway."

"If you don't mind my asking," Eva said, "maybe you can tell me why such a beautiful girl is a carpenter. Such heavy work. And a smart Italian girl, too."

It had never occurred to me to ask Rosie why she had become a carpenter. She thought for a minute. "I've always liked building things, making things. I like wood and I like houses and I like creating an environment."

"Ah," Eva said. "Creating an environment. A home, you mean?"

"Homes, offices..."

"A home," my father said, nodding.

"When I was a little girl," Rosie continued, "I liked playing with hammer and nails and saw. My father had some old tools. He wasn't very handy, but he had that much. We were kind of poor, then, and there were a lot of toys my parents couldn't afford to buy me. I wanted a playhouse when I was about eight, my father couldn't build things, and a playhouse would have cost a lot to buy, so I built one. Old scrap lumber, cardboard. I didn't have any roofing materials, of course, so I kind of shingled the roof with aluminum foil. It leaked." She laughed. "My mother found me a plastic tarp and I tied it down and nailed it every which way. I had to keep replacing pieces of the house, but I kept it together through the first two months of winter rain."

"Rosie grew up in Napa," I explained. She had never told me about the playhouse. Only the scooter that didn't steer.

"You made a house," Eva smiled approvingly. It wasn't cooking or sewing, but it would have to do.

We all had a little more wine. Eva was smiling and glowing, and my father had that silly look he got whenever he had a drink of any kind. That look brought back memories of family weddings, when my father, high on his one whiskey and ginger ale, would dance with my mother, swinging her around and shouting, "Look at her. So beautiful. So cute. Look at those fat little cheeks. Isn't she cute?" I wondered if he did the same with Eva.

Eva said dinner was ready any time, so we all sat down at the table, across the room from the fireplace. But Rosie sat for just a second, then hopped up again and followed Eva into the kitchen, to help. Then I jumped up and followed Rosie. My father stayed seated.

I carried the plate with the roast on it, Rosie carried the potatoes and carrots, sieved out of the gravy. Eva carried the gravy and the brussels sprouts. I went back for the root beer, diet and regular, and again for the bread. Rosie went back for the bean salad.

"For dessert," Eva said, "I got a cheesecake."

We all stuffed ourselves. Between bites, we talked about this and that. Eva was very good. We were half an hour into the meal before she asked Rosie if she was engaged or anything.

Now, I knew that Rosie had been seeing someone for quite a few months, but I also knew that they hadn't decided how far the relationship was going to go. My biggest concern was that Rosie would want to live with the woman and would decide the cottage was too small. I'd have to add a room to keep her around.

"Not engaged," she said. "But going steady."

Eva shrugged. She wasn't impressed with "going steady." She liked Rosie, I could tell, and until she actually married someone, she was a possibility for me.

"And what does he do?" Eva asked, hoping his status would be even lower than mine, whatever mine might be.

"Social work," Rosie said, avoiding pronouns. Rosie's not the kind of person who hides what she is, and she never lies about it, but neither is she interested in discussing her personal life in detail. When it comes to old people, if she thinks explanations might confuse or upset them, she tends to avoid the explanations.

"A social worker." Eva swallowed a piece of potato. "They don't make much money, but it's nice to do that, I suppose."

My father, who had worked for the WPA as a young man, was winding up, I knew, for a paragraph or two on poverty, welfare, and hard work. He took a swig of diet root beer.

"They don't know what it is, today, to be poor. All this welfare. They should be out fixing the streets, like I did. They don't know. I wouldn't wish another Depression, but they should know what it's like."

"Pa, I think some of them do know."

"People shouldn't go hungry," he said. "Not a dog, not a cat should go hungry." He looked down at Euphrates, who was waiting patiently beside the table for the plates to be cleared, grunting from time to time with food lust. Tigris was sitting on the chair near the fire, glancing our way frequently. Alice was sleeping on the couch. "But a man should have the desire to work." Was this an oblique criticism of me, I wondered?

Rosie got him talking about the Depression and the WPA. Once, when we'd known each other for only a short time, she had taken me on a tour of all the government-sponsored, Depression-era WPA murals in the metropolitan Bay Area. I think it was my appreciation of those murals that made her decide I could be her friend.

We cleared the table, just Rosie and I, and did the dishes, and then we all had coffee, caffeinated and decaffeinated, and cheesecake. My father was, by now, wild about Rosie.

When she got up to leave, he insisted on walking her to the cottage, despite the fact that she had a canine escort.

Later, after Eva had gone to bed, my father and I sat out on the front steps looking at the stars.

"A beautiful girl, that Rosie," he said. "But after all..." he nodded sagely. "We have to understand that we are in San Francisco." My father, man of the world.

I looked at him. He looked back at me slyly.

"Actually, Pa," I told him, "we're in Oakland."

SIX

My FATHER was sitting at the kitchen table drinking his morning coffee and reading the paper. Eva was in the bedroom making their bed. I had already made my couch, drunk one cup of coffee, made a phone call, and toured the yard. The ivy was strangling the acacia again. I would have to call someone to take care of that, since I was a busy man.

Eva finished the bed and joined my father in the kitchen. I hung around the living room, thinking about a second cup of coffee.

"What kind of person would do such a thing?" my father shouted. "They won't bury the dead people!"

Eva clucked. I really wanted that second cup of coffee. I strolled into the kitchen, hoping to avoid conversation.

"People are putting them in their refrigerators, maybe?" he cried. Eva clucked some more. I could tell that she, like my mother before her, was used to his enraged daily commentary on the state of the world, and just let him get through the paper pretty much on his own. Today's topic number one was a local cemetery workers' strike that was causing large-scale storage problems.

"Such a thing." He spoke this last more quietly, passing on to other news.

I got a clean cup. Eva had already washed everything used so far that morning. I poured reheated coffee.

"Who cares about such dummies?" he muttered. I put sugar and milk in my coffee. "If they're so stupid they shoot themselves full of poison—look at this, Jake, it's not bad enough they got the real thing, now they're making heroin in test tubes and they got these dummies getting sick from it. They got a name for it—designer drugs, yet. Such a thing." I clucked and shook my head. "And look here, in Berkeley, they got some son of a bitch breaking into houses and beating up old people, they think he's a dope fiend." I shook my head sadly and made my way out of the kitchen, cup in hand.

"Killing each other at ball games!" he yelled. "Those crazy people in Europe. Grown men kicking a ball, no wonder they kill each other."

I remembered the routine from my childhood. It was his way of dealing with an insane world. If the news items he raged about were stories of insanity, then there must be some sanity somewhere, even if only in his mind and in the minds of other right-thinking people who could see that these things were insane. He had never explained this to me; in my adolescence, in an attempt to make sense of the apparent insanity that was my father, I had developed that explanation myself.

Rosie was working that day, Friday, and was planning on working Saturday, as well, to hurry along the garage-turned-master-bedroom. On Sunday, she had unbreakable plans with the social worker. She might, she had told me, be available some time on Monday—certainly by Tuesday. I was working alone for a while yet.

I sat on the front step, drinking my coffee, half-tuning out the occasional verbal explosion from inside and laying plans.

I had an appointment to see Joe Durell, Noah's health food partner, on Saturday. I'd wanted to see him sooner, but he had begged off, saying he had too many appointments. He wanted me to come on Monday, but I pushed until he admitted he would be in his office the next day and agreed to let me come.

So I thought I'd spend some time tracking down information about Marjorie. At this point, that seemed like a good way to begin tracking down Noah. She hadn't left a spouse and a leaderless cult behind. If they had run off together, after all, I figured he might have covered his trail better than she had.

I finished my coffee and left the cup in the sink for Eva—why should I argue if someone wants to wash my dishes?—and left the folks poring over a map of San Francisco. They had rented a car the day before and were laying elaborate touring plans.

I took a walk down to the corner. Work was going along just fine on the ark. Laborers were hanging all over the hull like barnacles. Arnold was standing around supervising.

"Hi," I said. "How's it going?"

He shook his head. "Okay. We're moving ahead really fast now. But we won't be able to go on for long before we run out of money. Our people are getting worried. I'm afraid they'll lose faith if we don't find Noah soon." He spread his hands helplessly. "What should I tell them?"

I had not been hired to do public relations, but I took a stab at it. "Tell them what you think is happening."

"That there's been foul play? That we have someone investigating? That we're going ahead with the project in Noah's name, with all expectations of his return?"

That was good, standard stuff, I thought, vaguely familiar, slightly pompous, reassuring.

"I guess. Meanwhile, I'm moving right ahead on this, and I need something from you." He cocked his head, attentive, suspicious, terrierlike. "Everything you can tell me about Marjorie. Her background, her friends, that kind of thing."

He sat down on a pile of lumber. I joined him. Someone revved up the generator, plugged in a circular saw, and began slicing through two-by-twelves. A dozen hammers continued to whack away at the ark; someone dropped an armload of boards on the half-finished deck.

"Maybe we could go somewhere else?" I asked.

"I don't have that much to tell you. A few things. But Beatrice was a friend of hers, I think, and you should talk to her."

I looked around. "Is she here?"

"Not yet, but any time now. Let me think." He struck a thinking pose. The saw whined and shrieked. "I don't know much about her friends, except there's a boyfriend. Beatrice would know more about that. And some relatives here in town. I think she was born in Oakland. I can't remember whether it was the East Oakland ghetto or the West Oakland ghetto, but I remember her saying something about a ghetto."

"What does she do for a living?"

"Nursery school? Kindergarten? Something to do with little kids. Child care?" The saw was silent; the hammering seemed to get louder.

"How did she get involved in this?" I waved my hand at the general surroundings.

"Beatrice." As he said her name, she appeared from around the back of the ark. "Here she is," Arnold said superfluously, and waved at her. She smiled and walked toward us.

"Jake!" She was glad to see me. That was worrisome.

"Jake needs to know some things about Marjorie," Arnold explained. "I told him you were the one to talk to here."

"Of course, whatever I can do," she said. "I was just going to get some breakfast."

"Okay then, let's go," I said gallantly and with some misgivings. We walked back toward my house, where my car was parked at the curb.

"This is an old car, isn't it?" she asked uncertainly.

"It's a 1953 Chevy Bel Air," I told her proudly, unlocking the passenger side door. She stepped up and in without so much as remarking on the comfort of the seats.

I didn't wait to close the door after her, but walked around to the driver's side. I didn't know about Beatrice, but most of the women I go out with are not flattered by the helpless damsel treatment. Although they may not be prepared to smash the lock and get into the car on their own, they seem to prefer to close themselves in.

I slid behind the wheel. Beatrice was tugging on her door, grunting. "It's heavy," she said, managing at last to close it. It wasn't quite latched. I reached across her lap, awkwardly, reopened the door, and, with more intimacy than I liked, pulled it solidly closed.

"Anyplace in particular you'd like to go?"

"There's that bagel place on College Avenue," she said.

"I know it well." I pulled away from the curb, making a U-turn and heading northeast toward College, a street I think of as the Oakland Trail, over which the Berkeley chic have trekked to create outposts in the wilderness.

There are those who disapprove of this gourmet imperialism. There are purists who insist that Oakland is not Oakland unless it is aggressively unpretentious. And there are some who are afraid that if Berkeley chic is allowed to move in, an intrusive government of the politically self-righteous, like Berkeley's, will be close behind.

But I grew up in Chicago, and the big-shouldered, ugly, slob-town image just doesn't appeal to me very much. The East Bay has genuine vitality. It doesn't need to prove anything by walking around with its fly unzipped and grease spots on its tie.

Miraculously, I found a parking place a block from the restaurant.

There was a line at the counter inside, which meant we had to stand for some time next to the display cases near the door, the ones with the tortes and puddings and cakes sitting all pretty in little dishes with doilies under them. I gazed at the fudge cake until I stared it down, then transferred my gaze serenely to a plate of scones. When our turn came, I ordered one with milk. Beatrice checked out the big menu on the wall and asked for lox and cream cheese on a whole wheat bagel. There is no such thing as a whole wheat bagel; they should call it something else.

We carried our trays into the large, white-painted, squeaky-clean eating area. The place displays the work of local artists of various kinds. At the moment, the south wall was covered with framed needlepoint and the north with photos of people doing physical labor.

Beatrice took her plate and cup off her tray and leaned the tray carefully up against a table leg. I did the same. She fiddled with the alfalfa sprouts that formed a nest in her cream cheese, forked the lox into a more comfortable position thereon, and took a dainty bite.

I ate my scone, noticing too late that it had raisins in it, and drank my milk.

I filled her in on what Arnold had told me.

"West Oakland," she said. "She's from West Oakland. Not far from the Amtrak station."

"Where did you meet her?"

"A computer class. At Vista College." I'd been tempted once or twice to take a class at one of the community colleges, but had somehow never managed to do it. Beatrice, clearly, managed to do nearly everything.

"What do you do for a living?" I asked.

"I have some money," she said simply.

"I gather Marjorie did not? Have money?"

"No." She licked a dangling sprout off her lower lip. "Things were pretty rough for her, growing up. Poor. Rough neighborhood. Rough childhood."

"Tell me." I finished off the spotted scone.

Beatrice was not comfortable with open-ended challenges. She looked pained.

"Parents? Brothers? Sisters?"

"Her parents were killed when she was eight or nine. She told me they were just starting to get somewhere, her dad had a good job, they were thinking about moving somewhere nice. That's what she said, somewhere nice. But they were walking down the street one day and they walked near the wrong man. A dope dealer. A couple of other dealers in a big car drove by, shot at the rival dealer, and hit her parents."

"Shit," I said. They were calling them drive-by killings now. Every so often you'd hear about one. People shooting into the wrong car. Recently, in East Oakland, they'd managed to kill a little girl. The least they could do was get it right and kill each other. I noticed that Beatrice was looking startled, even a little disgusted, by my language. "Sorry. It just p—ticks me off."

She smiled. That was much better, she seemed to be saying. Jakie play nice.

"What happened to Marjorie after that?"

"She went to live with her grandmother. Not any money there, either, but a little house. A couple of years ago the two of them opened a daycare center in the house. They're doing well, Marjorie said."

"But she was taking a computer course?"

Beatrice finished off the last strip of lox, sipped her tea.
"She wanted to help her grandmother, but she wanted a
good job, too. And she wanted to move them into a better
neighborhood."

"Did she get a job?"

"She only took the one course. She was going to take
more, but she got involved in the arks. Noah's been paying her for some of the work she's been doing, kind of an
administrative assistant, I guess you'd call it. She did some
assignments."

"Like what?"

"Oh . . ." She looked vague. Since she was pale, with
blurred features and long light hair, her vague look turned
her very nearly invisible. "She did some liaison with the
Sonoma ark, and she talked to people who wanted to join
us. All kinds of things."

"Want some more tea?" She nodded and smiled shyly.
I got her some more tea, and a glass of water for myself.
It still seemed early for beer, but I was beginning to want
one.

"When did you last see her, Beatrice?"

"I saw her last Friday, the day before Noah left that
note. I saw her at the ark. We didn't have much chance to
talk, though. She said she had a bunch of things to do."

"Did she say what they were?"

"Oh . . ." The vague look again. "Some bookkeep-
ing—something about listing some supplies that would
have to be ordered. And some liaison work, talking to
people."

"How did she seem? Pretty much as usual? Upset?"

"Normal. Happy. She likes keeping busy."

"Have you got her grandmother's address or phone
number?"

"Uh huh. At home I do, not on me." She was looking in her teacup, smiling slightly.

"Great. You'll be working on the ark tomorrow, won't you?" She nodded. "Maybe I can just drop by there and pick it up?"

She raised her eyebrows and looked at me coolly. "Of course."

I smiled warmly. I didn't want to lose her yet. "Arnold said there was a boyfriend. Do you know him?"

She relaxed again; she must have decided I was just playing hard to get. "I don't exactly know him"—she made the "know" sound carnal—"but I have met him. Carl Hinks. Carleton. Nice guy. But he isn't her boyfriend any more. She's more or less broken up with him."

I've had one or two of those more-or-less breakups. They're usually terminal.

"When did that happen?"

"Gee, it's been a good month now. She just got busy with other things, you know, and she didn't have so much time for the things they had in common."

"Like what?"

"Like the Guardian Angels."

"You mean those Robin Hood gangs?"

"Well..." She looked doubtful. "I guess. You know, they try to protect people, clean up neighborhoods, scare off crooks. They don't steal or anything. Didn't Robin Hood steal? Marjorie would never steal. We wouldn't have anyone on the arks who stole."

"What happened between her and her boyfriend, exactly. Do you know?"

"Well, it's like I said. See, Carl's a Guardian Angel. So is Marjorie. But even though she's still one, she doesn't do a lot of that any more, because of the arks. There was some trouble about that. Carl said all she ever did was work on the arks, and he thought she should be doing what she was doing before. Helping protect the neighborhood. Fighting crime. He said that was where her duty lay, not with the arks. They used to argue about it."

I was on Carl's side. "She was a Guardian Angel. Her boyfriend was a Guardian Angel. Together they fought crime and injustice. Working side by side they made the city streets safe for you and me. And she gave all that up to build an ark? Was she involved with Noah?"

Beatrice's hopeless passion for me was fading fast. She just didn't appreciate my humor, not to mention my prose. She was indignant.

"No, she was not. She believed in the ark. Carl wanted her to patrol West Oakland. We're trying to save the whole human race."

I was beginning to feel cranky. Zealots can be very boring. "You don't have room for the whole human race."

"We have room for some of the best, and then we can reproduce."

"What about animals?"

"We're not taking those. God says humans can't be trusted with animals. He'll take care of that end of things."

I started to go after that interesting thought, but decided it could wait. The crawling roots of ark-people philosophy could go off in a thousand directions, none of which had much to do with the problem at hand.

"Where can I find this ex-boyfriend?"

"He works at the hat store up on Telegraph, the one near Dwight."

I knew the place, in Berkeley, near the campus. "And his name's Hinks?"

"Right. Carleton Hinks."

I drove Beatrice back to the ark site, promising to get back to her if I needed anything. Whatever that meant.

SEVEN

THE HAT SHOP was a narrow storefront that stretched back maybe thirty feet into dimness. There were three people in the place, two browsers and a young black guy standing behind a counter near the door. About twenty-five years old, narrow handsome face, skin the color of milk chocolate, hair very short, dressed in 1950s drag. Baggy pants with pleats. A pink shirt that looked just like the one I had when I was about twelve, the one I wore with my charcoal gray suit.

"You Carleton Hinks?"

He looked me over. His eyes rested for a second on my "Visit Lake Tahoe" tee shirt. "Sure am."

"Jake Samson," I said, extending my hand.

"I don't do the buying here," he replied.

I explained that I was not a hat salesman, that I was helping out at the ark, trying to get a line on Noah and Marjorie. He looked at me more carefully.

"I don't know what I can tell you, man. I don't know where the hell she is." He sounded like he wished he did.

"Maybe you can give me some leads. I don't know. But I hear you know her pretty well, and I've got to talk to anyone I can."

One of the browsers got serious and came up to the register with a straw boater. Carleton rang up the sale, bagged it, smiled at the customer, and said thanks. "Okay, I'll be happy to tell you what I can. But I can't really talk here." Another customer stepped up to the counter.

"Have you had lunch?"

"Yeah." He made the sale. "I get off here about six, but then I got to go take care of some business. You can meet me there if you want."

"Where you're doing business?"

"I'll just be sitting around. Looking out for some people."

"Guardian Angel work?"

"Yeah, that's right. You know about that, then."

"Where will you be?"

"You know the guy that's been breaking into houses over in West Berkeley, beating up old people, taking their money and TVs and stuff?"

I remembered hearing my father yell about it. I nodded.

"Well, some of us are staking out the neighborhood, you know? Housesitting. Making it easy for him to break in where we're waiting."

"I thought you people just patrolled the streets."

He flashed a cynical but charming smile. "We do what the situation calls for." He wrote a Tenth Street address on a scrap of paper and handed it to me. "I'll be there from eight o'clock on. Come at eight. The robber works later than that."

I told him I'd be there.

I spent the afternoon wandering around Telegraph, bought some jeans and a shirt, had a cup of coffee, stopped in at the framing shop and looked through the prints, and went home to a quiet and wonderfully empty house. Pa and Eva had gone out to dinner and a movie. I pulled a TV dinner from the freezer, wondering briefly how long it had been in there, watched the news and a couple of game shows, took a long, thoughtful bath, and headed for West Berkeley at 7:45.

The house was a small, scruffy Victorian cottage, in need of paint and even more in need of a little yard work. There was one light on somewhere in the back of the house, and the dim porch light barely illuminated the front door. I knocked.

A long thirty seconds later, the door opened. Carleton invited me in with a curt jerk of his head. He was still wearing the pleated pants, but the rest of him was dressed in the group uniform, Angel beret and shirt. I followed him through a tiny entry hall, a living room overfull of shabby stuffed furniture upholstered in ancient green brocade, and into a kitchen lighted only by the overflow from a tiny bedroom lamp in the next room. We both sat, on plastic kitchen chairs with chrome-plated legs. Carleton took a slug from a half-empty bottle of beer that he'd left on the table.

"How many of those have you got?" I asked chattily.

His head shot up from his contemplation of the bottle. "Hey, I can drink just one of anything."

"I didn't mean to offend you," I said, somewhat startled. "I was just hinting that maybe there's one for me."

He stared at me for a moment, then laughed quietly, embarrassed, got up, opened the refrigerator door just far enough to slip his hand inside, and took out another bottle for me.

"Sorry. Pretty rude. See, my old man drank himself to death, and I'm a little touchy. Matter of fact," he shrugged, "I'm a little touchy in general, okay?"

"Okay with me," I told him. "I suppose you're pretty touchy about Marjorie, too." I spoke in a near-whisper, following his lead.

"No."

"I thought she was an ex-lover. I thought everybody was touchy about those. The recent ones, anyway."

"Depends on the ex, don't you think? I mean, how it went bad, how it was good."

"Then tell me. How do you feel about Marjorie?"

He didn't so much as blink. "I love her. She's great. She never lied to me, never cheated, never fucked me over or fucked me up. She hurt the shit out of me, but that's how it goes sometimes."

"You mean when she left you for Noah?"

He shook his head. "She didn't leave me for Noah. She didn't leave me for anybody. She left me because she didn't love me in the right way, that's all. I don't even know if she and this Noah dude got something going. If it happened, it happened after we broke up, and she never mentioned it to me."

I thought about that for a while. I couldn't get anyone to say they knew that Noah and Marjorie were involved.

I pushed harder. "You sound a little altruistic. You always so sweet about getting dumped?"

There was that cynical smile again. "Nothing sweet about me. Marjorie, she's my friend." He paused. "You think I might have something to do with Marjorie going away? You think maybe I'd hurt her? I'm going to tell you something, Samson. I went with a girl once, she lied, she cheated, she even tried to steal from me at the end. And then she just walked out on me with this dude she'd been seeing for months and months.... I'll tell you something about that. I wanted them both dead. I wanted to take a gun and shoot her, and shoot him, and watch them bleed. That's how bad it was. That's how much hate she left inside of me. But I didn't do anything. It's been three years now, and I still wish, sometimes, that I could shoot them both. Dead, like they never lived at all. You ever feel that way? I was a dumb trusting kid and I didn't know any better, and she poured shit on my head and so did he. But

Marjorie? No. Not Marjorie. And I'm going to be more than a little bit upset if I find out someone has hurt her."

I didn't comment on his speech. I decided to change the subject for a while, just to ease things up a little.

"You alone here?"

"No. Got a partner. Out in the backyard. That guy starts to come in a window, we got him between us."

"How come you left a light on in there?"—I nodded toward the bedroom—"and the porch light?"

"Dark house is too suspicious. He don't mind somebody being home, and if she was home, she might be watching TV in the bedroom. If she's out, she'd still leave a light on. Nobody goes away and leaves a dark house. Maybe he even hopes she'll be here. She's an old lady." He looked as though the beer had gone bad in his mouth.

"Where is she?"

He smiled. "Some of the neighbors are having a party, so we got half a dozen empty houses tonight."

It took some effort to get back to the subject, back to the case I was working on, sitting as I was in the middle of an ambush. I found myself hoping the robber would show up. I was tired of thinking, of talking to people. A shot of adrenaline would be welcome.

"You say you and Marjorie are friends." He nodded. "I need to find her. I need to find out what's happened to her and Noah."

He brushed me away with a wave of his hand. "You don't care about her. You're looking for Noah."

"I was hired to look for Noah, that's right." I didn't start whining around about how of course I cared about Marjorie. I probably would if I knew her. She sounded like someone I might like. But I didn't know her, and my caring, if I could dig any up, was pretty abstract stuff. "But if I find Marjorie, I figure that will at least put me closer

to finding Noah. I thought she might have said something
to you before she went, might have given you some idea of
where she was headed."

He shook his head. "It was really kind of strange," he
said. "She never said a word to me. Not where she was
going, or even that she was going somewhere. I expected
to see her on patrol one night and she just didn't come.
Just never showed up. That's not like Marjorie, man. She
really cares, you know? She does her job, does her duty."
He swallowed the rest of his beer. I'd finished mine. He
didn't get another one for himself or offer me one.

"What night was that? The night you expected her to
show and she didn't?"

"It was last Saturday. I guess that's the first night she
was missing."

"Was she around the night before?"

"Huh uh. But she wasn't supposed to be on duty then."

"You say she always does her job. I heard you two were
having some disagreements lately about just that—she was
spending a lot of time at the arks and not doing the job you
thought she should be doing."

"We worked it out. She couldn't do it as often, but she
always came when she said she would."

"So I guess you're pretty worried about her?"

"Well . . . I'd be a lot more worried about her except for
one thing. Two things. First of all, she's Marjorie. Second, she's got this uncle or cousin or something. Victor.
When she didn't show up and I couldn't find her, I went
over to talk to Victor. And he said he thought he knew
where she was, but he wasn't supposed to tell anyone. Or
maybe he just thought it was none of my business, since he
never liked me. Anyway, he said up north somewhere. So
her family, they maybe know where she is."

In the second of silence that followed this, he held up his hand and cocked his head, listening. I stopped breathing. I didn't hear anything. We held the silence. Then I heard it, a scraping sound. Tensed, ready, I looked at Carleton. He had relaxed.

"It's just the tree again. Big old tree out in back, a little wind, it rubs against the aluminum gutters."

I relaxed too, and pulled out my notebook and pen. "You said a relative named Victor. Victor who? And where can I find him?"

"I don't know his last name. Just Victor. Victor's Auto Wrecking over in West Oakland. Probably in the phone book."

I wrote down Victor's Auto Wrecking, Oakland.

"Now, I don't mean to rush you, Jake, but I think I better pay a little more attention to what I'm doing here. You can find me at the hat shop if you need anything, or if you find out anything. I'd kind of like to know she's okay." He gave me his home phone number, too. "Tuesday through Sunday at the shop, though. Maybe you want to come in again and look at the merchandise some time."

"Maybe I will."

"Lot of guys your age go for those berets we sell, you know? You might look good in one."

"I have one," I said shortly.

He flashed a youthful and handsome smile and said, "Well, there, you see?"

"Looks to me," I shot back, jerking a thumb at his head, "like a lot of guys your age go for berets, too."

He laughed softly. "Yeah, well, these are a little different. You want one like this?"

"Maybe. You want some help here tonight?"

"You're not trained. Besides, we're staying all night."

"The old lady is going to party all night?"

He laughed. "No. She's coming home at midnight. But we're staying."

"I've got work to do tomorrow. But I could stick around for a while, maybe leave when she comes home."

He shook his head. "Can't have people running in and out of here at that hour. That's prime time. If he's around tonight, he'll be out there somewhere around then, for sure."

"What if he mugs her on the street?"

"Not his M.O. He likes houses, likes to take what's inside. Besides," he grinned, "we'll be watching out there, too."

"The night has a thousand eyes," I muttered.

"But mostly I can't let you stay because you're not trained."

I gave up. We shook hands and I slipped out the front door to my car.

Driving home, I thought about some of the things he'd said. He really seemed to care about Marjorie, but I couldn't forget what he'd said about the other woman who'd left him. Even though it sounded like he'd had plenty of reason, the fact remained that his feelings about her, and her boyfriend, were pretty ferocious. Murderous.

He'd asked me if I'd ever felt that way and I hadn't answered him. Had I? I'd had a hard time getting over a sleazy marriage to someone who had, like his girlfriend, lied and cheated. But had I ever felt like killing her, or the slime she'd been sneaking around with?

I remembered the day I went back to talk about possessions—which ones I would take right then, which ones she could have, which ones I'd want when I settled in somewhere.

It had been only two weeks since I'd walked out. I remember thinking, two weeks ago this woman was still my wife, still the woman I'd married and lived with and loved. In that two weeks, I'd sworn to leave her to her lovers, gotten scared of the loss and decided to forgive her, and discovered that she didn't want my forgiveness, didn't want me to come back. I sat there in our living room, across from her. She was sitting in my favorite chair; I was on the couch.

She had that look. The one that means, "I can't wait to get this over with and get you out of here and get on with my life." The look that is so hard to believe, so impossible to take in, when it comes from someone who used to love you. The look that always makes you wonder if they ever really did. It's the final look. There's no coming back from it. She was talking to me and she was completely inside herself, protecting herself from my pain but not really caring about it, just wanting it away somewhere. I wondered if her face had always been that large and flat and square. Because she was different, now, I could really see her. The charm was gone; she wasn't turning it on for me any more. The illusion was gone. There was nothing looking at me but her naked face, and it was not a face I loved.

I hadn't wanted to kill her then. But months later, when the shock had worn off and the anger had set in, I might have had one or two little moments. . . .

EIGHT

YELLOW BRICK FARMS occupied an old dairy near Boyes Hot Springs, just north of the town of Sonoma, in the eastern part of the county of Sonoma. I drove north along 80 to Vallejo, up through Napa County, and over the line. I was remembering that a decade or more ago, there'd been an ark in this area, too, but an ark of a different kind.

It was a huge old hotel-restaurant that looked like the world's biggest riverboat, owned and run by an ex-madam. The place always seemed to be surrounded by animals—dogs, cats, chickens, even a goat or two—and was decorated inside like you'd expect an old-style whorehouse to be decorated. The ex-madam, a huge woman who inspired both fear and loyalty in her employees, could sometimes be seen lolling on her bed through the open door of a draperied room just inside the entrance. She could always be seen somewhere in that hotel, yelling at a waiter, watching a bartender, casting a businesslike eye over the clientele. It was a great spot to eat and drink, although I never stayed overnight there. I heard, not long after I moved to the East Bay from Marin, that Maria's had burned down and been relocated somewhere unlikely—was it Vallejo? I don't know. I don't know if it's anywhere anymore, or if she's even alive.

The Yellow Brick plant was big, without a yellow brick to be seen anywhere. It was built, rather, of red brick, a strange building material for earthquake-land, but one which nevertheless has a way of showing up in out of the way places.

The many-paned windows were clean; the gutters were plastic, and probably new in the last few years. There were pink geraniums planted beside the door that had OFFICE printed in neat white block letters over it. Tidy. An air of comfortable success. No flash, no hype. There were only two cars in the parking lot, a Corvette and a new white Toyota.

The woman behind the desk looked like a lot of women I knew in the early seventies, only a little better. Her hair was longish and dark brown, fuzzy around the ends. She was wearing a kind of peasant blouse and a long skirt with flowers all over it. I couldn't see the shoes, but I guessed maybe clogs, maybe sandals. I was betting she'd been with the company from the beginning and was very dedicated, and, to go along with the dedication, underpaid.

When she raised her eyes to me, I knew she'd been wearing the same clothes for a dozen years. She was somewhere between thirty and thirty-five. She had dark blue eyes. Her face was round and innocent.

"Hi. What's your name?"

I was suddenly transported back to childhood. "Jake," I said. "What's yours?"

"Doreen." She smiled. A nice smile that almost compensated for the name. Names that end in "een" always sound like cleaning compounds to me. The two exceptions are Arlene and Francine, for some reason. "Is that Jake Samson?"

I nodded.

"Great name."

"Thank you." I couldn't decide whether she was projecting sweet dumbness or sexual subtlety.

She pressed a button on the intercom on her desk. "Mr. Durell? Mr. Jake Samson to see you."

All that "mister" stuff didn't quite go with the laid-back, groovy atmosphere of the outer office and its inhabitant. Mr. Durell asked for just a few minutes, and I sat down on the old wicker love seat that occupied the wall across from the desk. The room was large and full of plants. I noticed no ashtrays on the tables. There was a braided rug in blues and greens on the floor, and framed posters on the walls. Posters of flowers, of sixties and early seventies groups—Creedence Clearwater Revival was one—and some drawings in the colorful fantastical style that looked, then and now, like the product of an acid trip.

Mr. Durell really did need only a few minutes. He buzzed and Doreen—had she called herself something like Willowsong Peacelove once upon a time?—gestured me through a door that was painted yellow. "Second on the left," she told me.

I wondered why I was so conscious of the time warp she represented. I loved the sixties and early seventies. I think I feel a little angry because that time passed so quickly. Or because it didn't deliver what it promised. Or because it sailed away on a drug dream and left a lot of people stranded in a time so unromantic and unformed that no one could ever hope to grasp its principles, if it had any.

Durell's office was big and comfortable, and didn't look anything like the reception area. It was carpeted in something industrial and had white-painted walls hung with a few nondescript framed prints. Landscapes, flowers in vases, that kind of thing. The desk was an elderly wooden one, the chair a new executive swivel, and there were two wooden side chairs, a tweed-covered couch, and a coffee table.

Durell stood up and smiled, extending his hand over the desk, gesturing generously at one of the wooden chairs, which wasn't any more comfortable than it looked. I noticed the framed diploma. He had a doctorate in chemistry. Another refugee from the toxic wasteland?

Durell didn't look like he'd ever felt stranded. He looked very much at ease in the eighties. He was in his mid to late forties, hair cut short but not greased. He was wearing a white shirt with no tie, and suit pants. On a coatrack near the door I saw the suit jacket and tie. He looked tired, and glad to sit down again after we shook hands.

"Nice-looking operation," I said. Businesspeople tend to like that kind of nonstatement.

He nodded. "Business is good. And getting better."

I cocked my head. "Oh?"

"We're one of the older companies in the business now, you know. Got a good toehold on the supermarket chains."

"No wonder you're busy, then. Lots of work, no partner."

Durell shrugged. "Would you like some tea or something, Mr. Samson?"

"Jake."

"Joe."

"I don't suppose you have any coffee?"

"Sure we do." He buzzed Doreen and asked for two cups of coffee. "She's my Saturday-morning secretary," he said. I supposed he was explaining why he had a receptionist on weekends, when no one else seemed to be around. Or maybe he was just bragging about the amount of work he had to do. Or, then again, maybe this was man-to-man stuff, and I was supposed to guess she was some kind of office wife.

I nodded and smiled my congratulations, which would cover any of the above.

Doreen came in carrying a tray with two cups of coffee, a pint of half-and-half, and some brown sugar in a mug. She smiled at me sweetly when Joe thanked her.

"About Noah," I said, when the door had closed behind her.

He fiddled with his coffee, adding cream and sugar and stirring slowly and deliberately. "I suppose you want to know what I think about this disappearance thing."

"I do. And I wanted to get a feel for this company—how it got started, who's been around the longest, what people's relationships with Noah are like. Standard stuff."

"Checking out the suspects, eh?" He laughed. "Well, to tell you the truth, I don't know what to say. I guess he must be in trouble somewhere. I know his wife thinks so. And she's probably right. I can't quite feature him running off, either. He's a solid kind of guy, in his way."

I caught the "in his way."

"Tell me about him."

He leaned back in his chair, gazed at the wall behind me, clasped his hands behind his neck, and began. "I've known the man for years. Knew him back in Houston, matter of fact.... When he got this idea, it sounded a little harebrained, to me, at first, but I had a lot of respect for him, for the way he worked. It sounded like he'd looked into it, like he knew what the hell he was talking about. So I did a little nosing around on my own, and things looked even better. I put a little cash in the hopper, Tom came out here and got things started. Did good right from the beginning. I came out to lend him a hand, been here ever since."

His eyes focused on me again. I waited.

"Tom liked to manage the raw materials end of things— you know, buying from the suppliers, keeping an eye on them to make sure they kept it clean, real organic stuff. That was important to Tom. Is important.''

"And you?''

"Well, hell, it's important to me, too. Reputation's everything in a business like this.''

"No pesticides in the carrot juice, right?''

"Not funny, Jake.'' He shook his finger at me.

"Sorry. And your role in the company?''

"I'm still a chemist. Always will be, I guess. I handle the supplements, the processing. Vitamins, mostly. The lab's my baby. Our vitamins are pure. No sugar. No preservatives, just the real thing. Of course, I'm also Tom's executive vice president. Since he's gotten involved in the arks, that's become a much bigger job than it was before. He just hasn't been around as much.''

"You say you think he's in trouble, but the evidence points to a runaway. With Marjorie. What's so impossible about that?''

He smiled slightly. "It's not impossible. Middle-aged man...but it just doesn't seem like him, pulling his money out while the arks are being built, taking off with some little girl. Maybe someone saw a chance to get hold of a lot of money and took it. I hate to think that's what happened. I hate to think his body's going to turn up somewhere. Maybe I'm wrong. Hell, there's not a man alive who can't be tempted. But then temptation can go more than one way.''

"You want to explain a little more about that?''

He took a last swallow from his cup, and looked inside to make sure he hadn't left any coffee. "Well, hell, Jake, there's a lot of possibilities. Look. This Marjorie Burns. She's with him, or took off with him or something. Right? So there are three possible scenarios as I see it. One, they ran off together. Two, she was with him when he got kidnapped or whatever and she got what he got. Or three, maybe she arranged what he got. Ever think of that?''

"It had occurred to me. I can see you've given the situation some thought. Do you have any reason to think she might do something like that?''

"Hell, no. Hardly know the woman. You said you wanted to get a feel for the company. How about a tour?'' He stood up. I swallowed the last of my coffee and got up too.

"But you do know her?''

"We've met, sure.'' He shot me a thoughtful look as we walked out his office door and started down the hall. "I suppose you'll think it's funny, a practical guy like me, if I tell you I've done a little work here and there on the arks, too.''

"I don't think it's funny.'' Not as funny as pesticides in the carrot juice. "Is that how you met Marjorie?''

He nodded. "This ark stuff, I thought it was a little strange at first. You know, scientist, businessman, moves to California and goes peculiar. But I don't know. I believe we really have screwed things up pretty bad, just like before the last flood. And I always believed in the Bible. I guess I just decided not to argue with a man who said he was having dreams of prophecy. You look into it a little more, Jake''—he chuckled—"you might be wanting a reserved seat yourself.''

"Could be. What about what he said in the note, that there was something he had to do?''

We stopped outside a solid wooden door with the word LABORATORY printed on it.

"I haven't seen the note. Heard what it said. Look at it this way, Jake, either way it happened, the note's going to read that way. 'I've got this thing to do. Very important.' If he was kidnapped, that's what they'd make him write so no one would try to go after him. If he ran off with this Marjorie, it's a sure thing he'd want everyone off his tail and he'd want to give his wife a chance to think he was working. I don't think the note means a damned thing one way or the other.''

I tended to agree with him, but the note was all I had.

He unlocked the laboratory door, swung it open, and switched on a light.

It looked like a lab. The only one I'd ever seen was the one I'd been forced to spend time in back in high school chemistry, but this looked something like the one I remembered. It had cupboards and racks of test tubes and shiny white countertops. There was a very professional-looking microscope, a gadget he told me was a mixer, a kilnlike object which was, it turned out, a "precision furnace," a big box he said was a "refrigeration unit." Burners. Beakers. All very clean and tidy, like no one ever worked there, a room about twenty-by-thirty with one small window and lots of fluorescent light. Over all, a lingering mixture of chemical odors I couldn't recognize, although I caught a whiff of pine cleaner.

"Nice," I said. "For vitamins?"

"Oh, we do a lot of things here. Quality control. Shelf-life improvement. Making mixtures, trying out drying times. A lab in a food factory is like a thumb nail on a thumb."

A very pristine thumb nail. "Do you make the little pills here?"

He shook his head. "We send them out to be pressed and bottled. Of course, powders are the coming thing, bigger than pills."

"It doesn't look like you're working on anything right now."

He turned out the light and relocked the door as we left. "You're right. I don't get much time in there anymore. We're just keeping the old product line on an even keel these days. I've even sent some work out to consulting labs. I've become a manager." He sighed.

We were walking down the hall again, past some unmarked doors. "Offices," he explained. The idea of offices clearly bored him.

"Which one is Noah's?"

He pushed open a door and showed me a room that looked like it hadn't been used in a long time.

"I'm afraid his office won't help you much," Durell said. "He hasn't used it in months."

"I'd like to take a look, if it's okay with you."

"Sure, go ahead."

The desk was empty. The file cabinet was full of purchase orders.

We walked on. "So," I said, "he hasn't been around in months? Since he started work on the arks?"

Durell did a half-grin. "We've had a few meetings. He's been coming by every couple of weeks to look through his mail." We stopped in front of a swinging double door. He pushed in and we entered what looked like the guts of the business, a series of big, interconnected rooms stuffed with conveyor belts and machinery.

"This first room, here," he said, "is where we make our flavored rice nectars. It starts out right over there, with those boilers and kettles. First you boil the rice and then it goes into that big blender over there...," he pointed at something that looked like a large industrial vacuum cleaner. "That breaks down one of the chains of the carbohydrates and liquefies it. Then it goes back into a kettle and the starter's pumped in. See what we're doing here is making the first stage of sake. It's fermented, but it's nonalcoholic. It's called amazake. I tell you, those Asians... anyway, that breaks down more of the carbohydrates, makes it sweet—just from what's in the grain." He pointed to two huge vats. "It goes and sits in those overnight. It's agitated and temperature-regulated. Then it's pasteurized, and the bran gets sieved out over there." I had begun to drift into a fantasy of Noah's body being disposed of in these vats, cooked, packaged, run along a conveyor belt.... "Then it gets pumped over to that tank, where the flavoring is added—we did some apricot yesterday—and then it gets pumped over to that big fellow over there."

I snapped myself back to attention to look at his "carousel filler," a collection of funnels where the glop was dropped into the bottles, plastic ones, which were then machine-capped. A conveyor belt took the little soldiers over to another work area, where the still-hot nectar was dropped into a cold water bath.

"After that," he said, "we put the labels on and put the whole batch in one of those refrigerators over there." I followed him along the conveyor-belt trail to another machine. "Here's where we slap the labels on," he said. He reached into a carton, pulled out a roll of labels and tore one off, backing and all. "Souvenir?" he smiled. It was the label for Yellow Brick Farms' Apricot-flavored Rice Nectar. Pretty. A rosy-cheeked, slightly Asian-looking farm girl holding a bushel basket full of apricots. I hate apricots. I thanked him and pocketed the piece of paper.

He pointed through a door to another room. "We do the dried fruits in there. Want to have a look at that?"

"Thanks a lot," I said, "but I have a few more things I wanted to talk to you about." He looked disappointed. "You sound like you really miss Noah's presence around here."

"Sure I do. We're a good team. Oh, I can keep things moving. He always relied on me anyway, but in a partnership, each man has his own area of expertise."

"Yeah," I said. "But what does any of that matter, with the world ending?"

He laughed an "oh, you rascal" laugh.

We were back in his office again. He glanced at his desk. A new phone message memo sat in the middle of his blotter. He set it aside, settling back in his chair.

"Now, about the world ending," he began. "Yes, there was the flood to consider. But Tom's not crazy, you know. You do know that?" I shrugged. "Anyway, he wanted to keep the business going. For the employees, for the cash flow."

"If he's dead, what happens to his share of the business?"

He seemed surprised by the question. "Why, it goes to his wife, of course."

"One more thing. Do you know his other partner, this Pincus guy up in Tahoe?"

"We've met." His tone and expression were noncommittal.

"You don't like him?"

"He's a smart businessman, runs a nice little casino." Not one clue to his feelings.

"You think he could have something to do with this?"

"You know what they say about lying down with dogs."

"You think Noah's picked up some fleas?"

He grunted. "I'll tell you, Jake, I wouldn't accuse anyone of anything. But I just don't know."

On my way out, I considered inviting Doreen for a beer to pump her about the company, but she wasn't around. The Toyota was no longer in the lot. Maybe some other time.

I stopped for half an hour at a place I knew in Glen Ellen, a reputed haunt of Jack London's, and had a beer by myself while I went back over the Yellow Brick road. The rest of the day was spoken for. I had gotten roped into an afternoon with the folks, which was okay, and Eva's niece, which might not be okay. After that, I had my own plans for dinner.

NINE

I STOPPED at the ark on my way home to pick up the information about Marjorie's grandmother. Beatrice wasn't around, but she'd left it with Arnold. It was just one o'clock when I walked up to the house.

Pa and Eva were sitting on lawn chairs reading copies of an East Bay weekly they'd picked up on a stroll along College Avenue after brunch that morning. They were wearing new straw hats of wildly different styles. His was a rakish cowboy hat with a small feather, hers a wide-brimmed fantasy with a bunch of grapes nestled among the brim. I thought of Carl Hinks.

"No bananas?" I asked. "No pineapple?"

"Carmen Miranda I'm not," Eva laughed.

"You're better looking," my father said.

"Speaking of good looking," Eva said, "it's too bad you got plans for tonight. Lee is such a lovely girl."

"I'll meet her," I said reasonably. "I'm going shopping on Telegraph Avenue with you."

"That's okay," my father said, grinning viciously. "The niece is staying over in Berkeley tonight. We're going touring tomorrow, then dinner tomorrow night before she goes home again to... what is it called, Eva?"

"Petaluma," Eva said.

"The whole weekend? That's nice," I said. "I can have dinner with you tomorrow, but I'm working during the day."

"Another one of your articles that never gets printed?" my father asked.

"That's right, Pa. Tell me, Eva," I added, just to make conversation, "what did you tell Lee about me?"

"About you?" She laughed. "Why about you? Lee comes to Berkeley, she's got friends. Two birds—me, her friends. Who said anything about you?"

I sighed. I was afraid it was going to be a long afternoon. Of course, I wasn't exactly surrounded by adoring women at the moment, anyway. My eight-month romance with Iris Hughes, the gorgeous psychotherapist, had finished evaporating that summer, and neither of us was watching when the last little bit of it disappeared into nowhere. I was still seeing Chloe Giannapoulos occasionally. She was my dinner date that night. But she'd become involved with her work and possibly with one or two coworkers at *Probe* magazine, and didn't seem to be showing much gratitude any more to the guy who'd introduced her to the guy who helped her get the job.

The funny thing about it was, we liked each other a lot. But Chloe, who was somewhere around forty years old, had a battered emotional history that wasn't very different from mine. Although she trusted me as much as she could trust anyone, she was pretty damned happy with her life just the way it was. Professionally exciting and emotionally independent.

And since I wasn't sure that wasn't the best way to live, after all, I wasn't about to argue with her. The way I look at it, wait and see is always the best policy when it comes to love. Unless you've been hit with one of those swept away, don't-want-to-think-about-it, let's-do-it-now bombshells. In that case, you have a choice: be a damned fool or run like hell.

I haven't been faced with that choice in a long time. Maybe that's something you can do just so many times before the capacity to do it wears out.

I wasn't interested in falling in love; I wasn't interested in spending a lot of time with Eva's probably boring and unattractive relative. And even if this Lee was Aphrodite herself, she lived in Petaluma. I don't commute.

I had a few minutes. I repaired to my tiny office, which could best be described as a service porch, and started making lists of people to see and questions to ask.

She showed up about ten minutes later. I heard her arrive, and emerged from the back of the house with every intention of being cordial. Maybe even gallant.

If she wasn't Aphrodite, she could have passed in some circles. She was in her early thirties, I guessed, not too thin, not too fat. About five seven or eight. She had green eyes and red hair, not quite orange, a little deeper on the red side, very fine and soft-looking, cut short sides and back and longer on top. She had the redhead's pale skin, with a fine dusting of freckles across her nose. A nice nose with a small bump in it. Her mouth was spectacular: full lips and perfect teeth.

She was wearing pearl gray pants and a turquoise knit shirt that didn't have any animals on it. I have never liked turquoise. Suddenly I was crazy about turquoise, and redheads, and green eyes.

We acknowledged each other with fragile smiles. For one wild moment, I considered breaking my date with Chloe. But no, that wouldn't do. If you wear your heart on your sleeve, a woman will not let you take off your clothes.

I offered to drive our little expedition up to Berkeley.

Lee turned out to be perfect.

"I noticed this car when I drove up," she said. "It's beautiful."

I couldn't help myself. I opened the door with a flourish, guiding the older folks into the back seat. Lee stepped up gracefully into the passenger seat. I held the door until she was settled, then I closed it for her. I just couldn't help myself. I dashed around the gleaming blue hood and climbed in beside her, released the emergency brake and started the car.

"It sounds like it's in beautiful condition," Lee said. "And the interior is perfect."

"Rebuilt engine," I said. "Nearly original interior."

"Amazing," she replied, stroking the dash. That was almost more than I could stand. I shifted into gear and pulled away from the curb, trying not to smile like an idiot.

Eva, especially, was delighted with the street market, several blocks, on both sides of Telegraph, ending at the campus on Bancroft. Booths, tables, displays. I didn't know when the custom started, but I'd never known Berkeley without it. I also didn't know how the real stores on the street, the ones that paid rent, felt about the shopless commercial enterprises that flourished on their sidewalks every weekend, but I figured they were probably good for business generally on the street, and as "street artists," inviolable, essential to Berkeley's image of itself.

Some of the merchants actually were street artists, actually made the jewelry, cutting boards, little boxes, clothing. But a lot of the displays were run by employees of the businesspeople, many of whom were simply retailers. Right before Christmas, you could barely stumble down the sidewalks for the crowds of purveyors. Not a bad place to buy gifts, some of them handmade.

"Once," I heard Eva telling Lee, "when I was a little girl, I visited my aunt in New York, and she took me down to the Lower East Side. A marketplace outdoors, like this. Well, not like this, exactly. Same principle."

"Was a place in Chicago," my father said, "called Maxwell Street. Same thing. You could find anything. Antiques, even. But no more."

I reflected that Telegraph Avenue was a pretty sanitized version of either the Lower East Side or, especially, Maxwell Street, which I remembered vaguely from my Chicago childhood as a disintegrating, but still exciting, bazaar.

The expedition took a solid three hours, at which point it became time to go home and prepare for our various evenings. Eva came away with earrings and a scarf. My father bought a maroon tie with a hula dancer allegedly hand-painted on it. I don't know what stall he found it at; I missed it entirely. I hesitated over a tee shirt with "I Like Ike" printed on it, and decided not to buy. Lee bought a striped tank top that I would have loved to see her in right then and there.

On our way back to the car, I glanced toward the hat shop where Hinks worked, and decided I would stop in there, one day soon, and check out the merchandise.

Lee went back to her friend's house—who was this friend, anyway?—to change, and our little household took turns with the bathroom. I had to leave for San Francisco before Lee came back to get the folks, but Eva let me know that they, too, were going to The City to eat and see a show. "A musical," Eva explained, "because Lee knew we would like that. Such a wonderful girl."

I couldn't have agreed more, but I didn't say so.

Rosie was arriving home as I was leaving.

"I may be ready to start helping you on Monday," she said.

"Good. I need you."

"Yes, you do. Got a date?"

"Meeting Chloe."

"Say hi."

Less than half an hour later I was saying hi to Chloe at her Noe Valley apartment. A hug, a kiss on the cheek. Mutual murmurings of "It's been too long."

"Got any ideas about dinner?" I asked.

She had Haydn on the stereo; we were drinking a warm-up glass of wine, sitting on her blue overstuffed couch. Over in the corner was the rocking chair I remembered from her place in Novato, up in Marin County, where I'd first met her.

"I can't decide. I feel ethnic, but then again, sushi would be nice."

"What kind of ethnic, I mean besides Japanese?"

"My kind, dolt."

Greek food sounded terrific to me. It always does. "Know a place with belly dancers?"

The restaurant was out in the Sunset District, where the fog shows up earlier and stays longer than in other parts of San Francisco. I'd left Oakland in warm sunlight, wearing a lightweight shirt and sport jacket, carrying a pull-over. The fog got to the restaurant ahead of us; I put on the sweater as I stepped out of the car. Once the sun goes down, it's chilly everywhere. Occasionally, I still feel a twinge of nostalgia for those hot midwestern summer nights. But not often.

We passed through a door with a plaster relief of some Greek god, with fig leaf, stuck to it, entering a white-painted room with muted, varnish-heavy paintings of Greek scenes. A goatherd here, an Aegean harbor there. A Greek key design along the tops of the walls. We ordered retsina, salad, avgolemono soup, stuffed grape leaves, moussaka.

I asked her about work at the magazine, she said it was terrific, that she was expecting a promotion, that my friend

Artie Perrine, who had helped her get the job, was the "doll of the universe."

"He's married," I said. "He's got a kid."

"Not that kind of doll of the universe," she laughed. I didn't mention Lee, since there wasn't much to talk about yet. I told her about the ark people and the mystery of the disappearing Noah. She was intrigued.

"Sounds like it could make a story, depending on what's happening. If it's all a scam. Are there any investors? So-called little people?" I shrugged in ignorance. "Can you find out?" I told her I planned to.

"And then there's his disappearance. With his own money? I wonder. What about this health food business, anything there? Or Marjorie Burns and her G.A. friends?"

I informed her that I had some ideas developing, and that *Probe Magazine* would certainly hear all about it, if there were anything to interest *Probe Magazine*.

She poked away at me about the case, promising there'd be nothing in the magazine until I cleared it. If anything was ever printed at all.

The salad was good, especially the cheese and olives. The egg-lemon soup was a little thin, the stuffed grape leaves not stuffed enough, the moussaka the best I'd ever eaten. There was a belly dancer, all right, and she was good. And when she bumped and writhed her way over to our table, I stuck a dollar bill in her bra. She was even pretty, but she just couldn't match up to Lee.

Chloe and I spent a nice evening together, the kind of evening two good friends can have. I still thought she was pretty sexy, but she seemed, oddly enough, to be perfectly happy to be my friend.

On the way home, tired, overfed, wine-depressed, the five-mile limbo of the Bay Bridge's lower deck seemed too much of a price to pay for getting home. The bridge was built to emphasize the glory of San Francisco and the degradation of the East Bay. First of all, you have to pay to cross into San Francisco. No charge the other way. Implication: who'd pay to go to Oakland? Second and even more significant, you drive the upper deck west to San Francisco, the lower deck to Oakland. The significance doesn't lie only in the class distinction between upper and lower. The upper deck provides a view. You see magnificent S.F. in the distance, pass through the tunnel at Treasure Island, come out the other side to see magnificent S.F. suddenly closer, sprouting out of the Bay, coming on like an overstaged, overwritten Broadway musical. On the lower deck you see girders.

Same thing on the Richmond-San Rafael Bridge from the East Bay to Marin. The Golden Gate Bridge is a different story. Since it spans the Bay from Magnificent S.F. to Marvelous Marin, it has only one level: the upper. But should anyone try to forget what's what around here, you still have to pay to go from Marin into San Francisco.

I slithered across the Bay on the lower deck.

Ten minutes later, yawning, I pulled up in front of my house. Stretching, I stepped out of my car. A good night's sleep in the steel trap, that was what I needed.

Then, from somewhere up the driveway, came an eruption of shouting, snarling, and barking. The floodlight on the side of the cottage, suddenly on, backlighted a large, deformed, many-legged creature racing down the drive, tearing up gravel, followed by Rosie, yelling, running, and waving a poker.

The monster broke apart with a yowl. Alice fell back for a second, slowed by a blow or a kick, and the man, still large and on his own, crashed through the gate and through me. I caught him with a glancing punch, almost stopped him with a tackle that skinned my belly, and took

off after him, hearing Rosie still yelling, "Stop the bastard!"

He raced across Cavour; I was maybe three yards behind him and halfway down the block before I realized I'd
lost Alice because I'd neglected to give her permission to
cross the damned street.

I expected him to jump a fence, cut through a yard, pull
some kind of diversionary tactic, but he just kept running
in a straight line toward the next corner, where the sudden
start of an engine and glare of headlights confused me,
momentarily, on the dark and quiet street.

"Stop him!" I yelled optimistically, just before the passenger side door flew open and my quarry leaped inside. I
grabbed hold of the door handle and nearly had my arm
ripped off when the driver pulled a fast U and cut around
toward College Avenue. I sat in the street, massaging my
shoulder, saying foul things softly, catching my breath. A
couple of porch lights came on. A woman in a long plaid
robe asked, from halfway behind a door, if I was okay. I
said yes. A man called out from an upstairs window of
another house—did I need help? No, but thanks. Had
something happened? Should he call the police? The
woman said she had. I said I thought the people down at
my house probably had, too. I thanked them and started
trotting home.

I heard a siren. I arrived just as an ambulance pulled up,
followed by a squad car. I felt the blood drain out of my
head, then rush back in.

"Is somebody hurt?" I blurted.

The ambulance guys ignored me. The cop told me to
take it easy and who was I, anyway. I told her, as I dashed
up the driveway beside her. Rosie was there, and Alice, and
Eva, on the path beside the cottage. So was my father, but

he was on the ground, half sitting up, leaning on one elbow.

Eva was crying. Pa was telling her not to cry. The ambulance guys checked him over, put him on their stretcher, and started carrying him away.

"What's wrong with him?"

"Looks okay," they told me. "But he's got a head injury and he needs to be checked." They were going, they said, to Merritt Hospital. Eva went with him. The cop asked me to stay.

Rosie told her part of the story. She'd been asleep. Alice had growled, then barked, then hurled herself at the door just as Rosie heard someone cry out, heard a scuffle on the path. She grabbed a poker and opened the door, and she and Alice came upon the big intruder, kneeling over my father, his hands gripping the old guy's collar. Alice had gone for one of those hands, and as the man jumped to his feet, Rosie had swung at his head and missed. That was about when I'd arrived.

I told the cop about my pursuit and loss of the mugger, giving her a description of him that wasn't too useful. He'd been wearing jeans and sneakers and a dark sweater. He was white with medium hair, medium brown, medium length. He was big. The car? Old, big, dented on the passenger side door. Early seventies, I guessed. A General Motors car, I thought, dark blue. No front plate, but when it did the U, throwing me down, I caught an initial letter C. The rest was unreadable, smeared with something.

The driver? All I saw was a flash of blond hair.

She let us go to the hospital. Eva saw us walk into emergency and waved us to seats beside her. "I think he's all right," she said. "That's some neighborhood you live in."

They poked around a little and turned Pa loose. A bruise on the forehead, a grazed elbow from being knocked to the ground. He came out smiling. I drove everybody home.

"We live in Chicago so many years, and we have to come to California to get mugged," Eva grumbled, furious with him, now, in her relief.

I was wondering why someone attempting a burglary—the crime choice in that neighborhood—would have an accomplice waiting a block away. Kind of far to carry the TV and stereo.

Rosie said goodnight. Eva said goodnight. I wanted to get into the bathroom and have a look at some of my own wounds, but my father signaled that he wanted a word with me. We went back out onto the front steps. He explained that he'd gone into the yard to get some air before he turned in and that's when the man had come over the fence from the yard next door and jumped him.

"I didn't want to say with the women around," he whispered. "And I didn't know whether to say to the cops, either, without having talked to you first."

I nodded, not having any idea of what it was he was going to finally say.

"That guy, he was no mugger." A dramatic pause. "He said, 'Okay, Samson,' and then he knocked me down. Then he was staring at me when your tenant and Lassie came running out."

I didn't say anything.

"So he was after you, big shot. You steal his girl or something?" I could tell by his tone of voice he didn't believe that.

"Not exactly," I said.

"You know, I been wondering about these articles that never get printed."

"There's nothing to wonder about, Pa. Nothing to worry about, either."

"Maybe you do something you can't talk about?"

"I don't know what you mean."

"Sure, sure. It's okay, Double-O-Seven. Just be careful. And I told Eva we don't need to say anything to Lee. She'll worry. And she don't need to know you got funny business."

Not knowing what else to say, I said goodnight.

TEN

EVA AND MY FATHER, despite the excitement of the night before, were up at their usual seven a.m. Sunday morning, which of course meant that I was up as well.

I heard my father leave the house and come back moments later. I opened my eyes. He was carrying the Sunday paper, which he'd picked up at the front gate. He took it into the kitchen and dropped it on the table. Eva ran water into the tea kettle for about an hour. The toaster ka-chunked down to On. I got up.

Lee, Eva informed me, was arriving at nine.

I drank some coffee. They ate a couple of slices of toast. My father grunted briefly through the news section of the paper. Then he invited me to take a walk. "Just a little one, maybe around the block."

"Doesn't your head hurt?"

"Nah. A little bump."

We had barely hit the gate when he looked at me slyly and said, "I suppose you can't talk about your work?"

"Pa, I'm not a spy."

"So what are you?"

"I don't want to talk about it."

"It's that bad? I should call you Mr. Capone?"

I gritted my teeth and shook my head.

"So who wants to bump you off, huh? Tell me that, big shot?"

"Nobody wants to bump me off. He was a mugger. Forget it."

We had gotten as far as the corner. My father stopped, and, in the way of all sidewalk superintendents, planted his feet firmly, stuck his hands in his pockets, and gazed at the ark workers and their work from under the brim of his cowboy hat.

"You want to change the subject? Okay. I'll change the subject. The neighborhood's always this noisy?"

I denied it. "Just a little building project. You know, a boat."

He cocked his head at me. "Little. Hah. Houses I've seen. Office buildings I've seen. Condominiums I've seen. Boats I've seen. They say it's a boat. Your friend Rico says it's a boat. You say it's a boat."

"It's a boat. You've met Rico?"

"Sure. He comes to watch. We talk. Nice fellow. He likes you."

"Does that surprise you?"

He shrugged. "What's not to like? So, this boat, they're going to put wheels and a motor and drive it to the ocean?"

I gave up. I told him, in the most general terms, about the ark project.

He nodded soberly. "I have heard that people do things like this in San Francisco." He turned back to look at the ark, nodding in a way I knew well, a way that meant something was about to be set right, corrected, explained. At that moment, Arnold saw me and waved. I waved back.

"Of course," my father said. "Forgive me. These are your friends."

"I've talked to them," I said, "about the noise."

"You should talk to them about their ark." I had known it was coming, and here it was. School time. "I sent you to Sunday school. You don't remember anything?"

"A little." Mostly I remembered Marcia Goldberg. She was beautiful.

"You don't remember that God promised he would never send another flood? That he made a covenant with Noah that he wouldn't do it again?"

I hadn't remembered that, no, but I nodded. It didn't help. His right hand was out of his pocket, his index finger raised in the rabbinical manner. Point one was about to be made.

"God said, 'I will establish my covenant with you; neither shall all flesh be cut off anymore by the waters of a flood; neither shall there any more be a flood to destroy the earth.'"

Neither had I remembered that my father could quote endless passages from everything he'd ever read, including *Time* magazine.

"I guess these people think that's changed somehow," I said.

"And he said in his heart, 'I will not again curse the ground anymore for man's sake; for the imagination of man's heart is evil from his youth; neither will I again smite anymore every thing living, as I have done.'"

"Well—"

"And," the index finger would not be deterred. "God told Noah how big he should make the ark. He said, 'The length of the ark shall be three hundred cubits, the breadth of it fifty cubits, and the height of it thirty cubits.'" With a final emphatic poke at the air, the finger crashed, with the rest of his hand, against his thigh. "You going to tell me that thing is three hundred cubits long?"

"No, I'm not. Because I don't know how long a cubit is, or even what it is."

"A cubit is from my elbow to my fingertips."

"Mine, too?"

"Smart guy. About a foot and a half, a couple inches more maybe."

Eighteen inches per cubit—maybe a little more—would make the original almost 500 feet long. I had figured this one for somewhere around 150 feet.

"They had to fit it on the lot," I argued. He snorted. "They're building more than one," I said, wondering why I was on their side.

"That ain't no ark."

"They think it is."

"It ain't no ark."

"You want to walk some more?"

"Sure. Maybe we can see somebody building the Brooklyn Bridge."

Lee was just pulling up as we rounded the corner toward home. She was driving a nearly new BMW.

The three of us walked up the driveway together. Tigris and Euphrates, lounging on my scraggly leaf-strewn lawn under the silver-dollar eucalyptus, yawned at us.

Even though she didn't ask, I explained that I had some work I needed to do that day, and would not be able to join them until dinner.

Eva was not quite ready to leave—she had cried out her hello from behind a closed bedroom door—so we all sat around the living room. I certainly wasn't about to go yet.

I asked what their plans were.

"I thought we'd do a little tour of The City. Chinatown, the Wharf, Golden Gate Park, then maybe go over to the Cliff House and watch the seals, have a glass of wine. You said you'll be able to have dinner with us?"

"Oh, yes, definitely. Where should we meet?" I now noticed that my father had slipped away, but I hadn't noticed where he'd gone.

"When do you think you'll be free?"

I wanted to visit Marjorie's grandmother and Victor's junkyard that day. I knew the junkyard was open because I'd checked it out by calling. I had not called the grandmother. I really had no idea how long the day's chores would take.

"It's hard to tell," I said mysteriously, "but I should be free by six." I expected to be free a lot sooner than that, but I didn't want to take any chances. Besides, busy is attractive.

"Then I guess the simplest thing would be to meet you back here and go on."

"You wouldn't rather eat in San Francisco?"

"Not particularly," she said. She smiled. Her green eyes had brown flecks in them. "I have to drive back up to Petaluma tonight anyway."

"Okay." I smiled at her. "I'll see you here around six, then."

"Yes. Around six..."

Eva came in from the bedroom. Simultaneously my father appeared at the front door. Lee turned to them, all business, and began to talk about the day's plans. I was no longer there, so I left.

ELEVEN

THE ADDRESS that Beatrice had gotten for me was a few
blocks below Market Street, just a mile or so south of the
Berkeley border. Poor to lower middle class, the main
streets infested with dealers, junkies, and punks, but the
residential blocks of small stucco houses, too many of
which had bars on the windows and doorways, were well
kept, the yards fussy in their neatness and respectability.

Mrs. Burns's pale green stucco was bigger than some of
its neighbors. It had a second story and a shallow front
porch. The front yard was solid juniper. Attached to the
porch on one side was a trellis overcome and sagging with
the weight and aggressiveness of a huge purple bougain-
villea with two-inch thorns. On the other side of the entry, lined up on the porch, was an array of cactus plants.
There were no bars on the windows. Maybe she thought
guard-plants and the BEWARE OF THE DOG sign taped
to the front door would do the job. Another sign, in the
window, said CHILD CARE.

I rang the bell, and a dog barked hoarsely. A moment
later, I heard footsteps coming toward the door. A curtain
at the front window shifted a few inches. A voice said,
"Who's there?"

I told the voice my name, and explained that Beatrice,
a friend of Marjorie's had given me her address; that I
wanted to talk about Marjorie; that I was a friend. There
was some hesitation behind the door, then it opened the
width of a chain. A dark wrinkled face looked me over
very carefully.

"What do you want with Marjorie?"

I explained that I was trying to find Noah, and that Marjorie was, apparently, with him. She nodded once and opened the door.

"Can't be too careful these days," she said.

"Absolutely," I agreed. There was, indeed, a dog, possibly one to beware of. He stood beside the woman mumbling toothlessly, his rheumy old eyes glaring at me, daring me to attack.

"His name's Francis," she said. "After the talking mule."

"Hi, Francis."

His tail swung slowly back and forth a couple of times. He limped arthritically out of the room. I never saw him again.

Mrs. Burns was a small, thin old woman with gray hair and a lot of lines around her eyes. She was wearing a longish navy blue dress with tiny white dots, and a pale blue bib apron, which she took off when she led me into the living room.

"If you'll excuse me a moment," she said, "I want to check on the kids before we settle in for a talk."

"Kids? On Sunday?"

"Not everyone works during the week, you know," she chided me. "The two I have on Sunday, their mama's a waitress." She walked quickly, but a bit stiffly, toward the back of the house. I heard a child giggle. She came back.

I had taken the offered seat on a brown plush couch, the likes of which I haven't seen outside an antique store since my grandmother died. The kind with tapestry cushions and claw feet. The plush was worn along the arms and back. The room itself looked newly painted in a cream color with brown trim. It was crowded with furniture: side tables, a three-tiered bric-a-brac table, a large easy chair with a footstool, a huge plastic recliner. The nine-by-twelve rug was a deep plum color and looked new. The room was warm and comfortable and smelled of lemons.

"You like the rug?" she asked.

"It's very nice."

"Marjorie bought it on sale."

"Recently?"

"Oh yes, just a month or two ago."

"I guess Noah pays her pretty well, then?"

She frowned at me. Not a polite question. "Our expenses are low. And he pays her just fine for the work she does, yes."

"Mrs. Burns, what do you think has happened to Marjorie?"

"Happened?" She gazed at me for a moment. "Why do you think something has happened to her?"

"The people at the ark think that Noah has been kidnapped. And he left a note saying she was with him. What do you think that means?"

"Mr. Samson, I'm sure I don't know. All I know is that she said she was going over to Lake Tahoe on some kind of business. She didn't say she was going with Noah. She's a grown woman. I didn't ask."

I had noticed a framed color photograph of a young woman on the three-tiered table. I got up and walked over to it. "Is this Marjorie?"

"Yes." She was beautiful. Very dark, with a wide, soft smile and strong, arrogant eyebrows. Her eyes looked calm—maybe a little hard?—and her hair was very short.

"When was this taken?"

"Oh, not even a year ago."

"Has she changed her hair since then?"

"No."

"Do you have another of these photos?"

"You want a picture of her?"

"Yes."

"I have a black-and-white you can have. If you won't lose it." She didn't like the idea, but my suggestion that Marjorie might actually be missing had worried her. "I'd like some coffee now. Can I make you some? Or would you like some soda? Marjorie likes that Napa Natural orange. We have some of those."

"I'd love one, thanks."

She wasn't gone long; the coffee must have been on the stove and the photograph within easy reach. She handed me a can and a glass, then the photo.

I poured. "I hope you don't mind these questions, ma'am," I said. "But there is some concern that Marjorie might be in trouble, or in danger, along with Noah."

"I see that now," she replied, just a bit impatiently, "but I still don't know why anyone would think that."

"Is it usual for her to go off for a week or more at a time?"

"Well, no. It's not something she does much."

"She works with you here. Isn't it hard taking care of everything yourself?"

"Yes. Yes, it is." She allowed herself to look just a little tired and put upon. For the first time, I realized she had to be in her mid-eighties. "And of course I wish she'd get back soon."

"The people close to Noah think he's been gone too long, too, and that he wouldn't have gone off that way and disappeared. They think the note he left was dictated by someone else. And he disappeared with a lot of money."

"What did the note say?"

"That he had something he had to do."

"Maybe he did." She sighed. Everybody had something to do and she needed help.

"Yes," I agreed. "Maybe he did." I drank some of the orange soda. "I don't know how to ask this, Mrs. Burns, but do you think there might have been anything going on between Marjorie and Noah?"

"You certainly do come up with some very personal questions, Mr. Samson." She sipped her coffee. "I don't think so. Or at least not so I noticed. She's out a lot. She works on the ark. She helps out that young Carleton Hinks, walking around the streets. Like I said, she's a grown woman, and I can't be worrying and wondering all the time. But I think I would have seen it if she was in love. When she was going out with Carleton all the time, she thought she was in love with him and it was plain to see in her face."

"What about Carleton? She broke up with him, right?" She nodded.

"How did he take it?"

"Kind of hard, she said."

"What do you think of him?"

"Seems like a nice enough boy. Maybe a little wild. Polite with me."

"A little wild?"

"Don't you think it's a little wild to be running the streets wearing shirts that say 'Guardian Angels,' pretending to be policemen?"

"You don't approve?"

"Oh, it's not that." She waved a large-knuckled, weary hand. "Somebody has to watch out for folks. The police sure don't, or can't, or maybe won't. I guess it's just too bad that somebody has to, and I guess I just don't like anything very much, or approve of anything very much, anymore." She looked at me with a tiny smile. "That's how old women talk, you know. It's because that's how we feel. Can't seem to help it."

"So I guess you didn't like Marjorie out there running the streets, either. Were you glad when she got involved with the arks, not patrolling so much?"

"Seemed safer, anyway. Crazy, but safer." She laughed.

"Did you ever meet Noah?"

"No. Never met none of them except that Beatrice. Funny, mousy little thing, but Marjorie said she was a good friend to her."

"This trip Marjorie was making to Lake Tahoe, did she say what it was about?" She shook her head. "Do you have any idea?" She shook her head again.

"I'm sorry I can't be more helpful. I just don't know."

"Had she gone to Tahoe before on business?"

She thought a minute. "No, I don't believe so."

"Mrs. Burns, it has been suggested that Marjorie might be responsible for Noah's disappearance."

She looked puzzled, then, as she understood, indignant. "You mean carried him off somehow, taking his money?" I shrugged, helpless and noncommittal. "No! That is not possible. Marjorie is not a criminal. She hates criminals. Her own parents were murdered by drug pushers. She's a good girl. I think everybody's going to feel real foolish when those two come back from their business trip." Her small dark face was darker, flushed with anger.

"I'm sure you're right." I hoped she was, anyway. I finished my soda. "Could I ask you one more question?"

"Well, I suppose so, but I hope you're not going to make me mad again."

"I don't think so. When was it Marjorie left, when she said she was going to Lake Tahoe?"

"Let's see . . . it was on a Saturday. In the evening. She called me, I don't know from where, and said she had to take a business trip to Lake Tahoe and she would be back as soon as she could. And not to worry."

I pulled out my pocket notebook and consulted it. Noah had left his note on the morning of Saturday, the 14th.

"Would that have been the fourteenth?" I asked.

"Was that a week ago?"

"Yes. A week yesterday."

"That's right, then."

"Had you seen her earlier that day?"

"Why no, as a matter of fact. She got up real early, before dawn, that day. Told me the night before she had some work to do first thing in the morning. Somewhere to go." She anticipated my next question. "She didn't say where."

A child started wailing at the back of the house. She stood up. I stood up, too.

"It was nice meeting you, Mr. Samson, but I have to go to the children now."

"I'll let myself out. Thanks. I'll call if...." She had already left the room.

TWELVE

VICTOR'S AUTO WRECKING was west of downtown Oakland in an area that was mostly warehouses and small, decrepit businesses, with a scattering of houses that looked like they were waiting to be jacked up and moved somewhere else.

The freeway ran overhead, shadowing the street, its steady hum muting the sounds of life below. The junkyard was next to a tiny restaurant that washed the atmosphere with lunchtime barbecue sauce. The smell was almost irresistible, but I had made the mistake of stopping for a fast-food burger on the way.

I pulled open the office door and stepped into a small dark room lined with shelves of mysterious objects stuck together with grease and age. The black woman sitting behind the dented metal desk looked up from a parts catalog and smiled. She had a kerchief over her hair and was wearing a light-colored smock she had somehow managed to keep reasonably clean.

"I'm looking for Victor," I told her. "My name is Samson."

"Yeah? Hope you're not going to pull the place down around our ears."

It was a joke I've heard too many times to count, but I smiled and dutifully recited my answering line.

"Not unless you try to cut off my hair."

She snorted. "Victor's out back." She got up. "You come after a part?"

"No, I was sent by Carleton Hinks, a friend of his. I need to talk to him."

She narrowed her eyes, looking a little less friendly.

"Okay," she said doubtfully. "Just go out through that door, turn right at the garage and then left. He's under the Gremlin."

The door she'd pointed to was a small, narrow side door no more than five feet tall. I ducked through it.

The sunlight was blinding after the dim office, and the air smelled almost fresh, compared to the acrid odors of old metal collecting dust on the shelves. I nearly fell off the plank walkway, set above the ground on concrete blocks, that led from the office door to the open double garage and off to the right.

The walkway seemed to serve two purposes. First, it provided a bridge over what must have been, in winter, a swamp of mud and grease. Second, it was a crooked but stumble-free trail through a jungle of fenders, bumpers, gas tanks, and crates of the same kinds of mysterious objects that were stored inside. The garage provided shelter for more of the same, as well as a Buick—1958?—with no wheels, no hood, and no engine. Besides the garage, Victor or someone before him had erected three small tarpaper sheds that I assumed held tools, or maybe car limbs and organs too delicate for the light of day.

I followed the walk around the garage to another, separately fenced yard wherein lay half a dozen vehicles of varying age, all missing vital parts.

I was stopped by the sight of a large tan dog, approaching me stiff-legged with suspicion. I spotted Victor's feet sticking out from under a Gremlin.

"Hi, pooch," I said. The phrase, "meaner than a junkyard dog" was running through my mind. The beast relaxed a bit, but my voice had been a signal. Another dog, a large tan female, strolled out from behind an ancient pickup truck that had no headlights and no grille. With her were two large tan pups, smudged with grease, rolling all over each other's fat little bodies in play. The female glanced at me and lay down. The male joined her. I reflected that Marjorie had a very doggy family.

Victor was still under the Gremlin. I spoke loudly to his overalled legs.

"Victor?"

"Yeah, just hold on a minute, man."

He did something to the car's underside that required two bangs and a grunt, and eased himself out into the sunlight, holding a wrench in his hand. He stood up and propped his butt against the fender.

"I'm pretty busy. What do you need?" He was short and stocky, about thirty-five, with acne-scarred cheeks.

"I'm looking for some information. Carleton Hinks said you might be able to help me."

"What kind of information?" His voice was neutral, his face blank.

"I'm looking for a man named Gerhart, Thomas Gerhart."

Victor shook his head. "Don't know him."

"He calls himself Noah."

"Oh, yeah," he laughed. "That crazy white dude. But I still don't know him.

I took out my wallet.

"Put that away," Victor barked. "What I mean to say is, I don't know the man. Not to talk to. Marjorie, she knows him. Don't know why."

"And Marjorie is your niece?"

"She's my cousin."

"When was the last time you saw her?"

He was still holding the wrench. He shifted it to his left hand and began tapping himself on the thigh with it. "I don't see that that's your business. You a cop, you show me your I.D."

"I'm not a cop. Noah's friends are worried about him. They think he's with Marjorie. I'm trying to find them. Just helping out, okay?"

"And Hinks sent you here?"

"He gave me your name."

"That boy's got a big mouth."

"Come on, man," I told him. "I'm just trying to figure out what happened. When did you last see her?"

He shrugged. "Before she took off."

"Which was...?"

"Week or so ago, I guess."

"Did the family report her missing?"

He was tapping the wrench against his thigh again. "Ain't no family, just me and her grandma. You mean report to the police?" He laughed. "Marjorie, she's been pretty much on her own since she was sixteen. I helped her out once or twice, but she don't take nothing from nobody, if she can help it. She's just that way." He shifted the wrench back to his right hand again.

"Do you think she would have run off with Noah?"

He sighed. "No way to know what she'd do. Look, I got work."

"So do I. Carleton says you think you know where they might be."

He shot me a hostile look. "Maybe Carleton's lying."

I gave him a look of my own. "Maybe she's in trouble. Maybe this time she needs help."

He backed off a little. "Uh huh. And what if she's doing something she don't want people to know about?"

"Look," I said, "that group of Noah's doesn't think he ran off. They think something's wrong."

He shook his head. "Right, Samson. And they think they're going to sail away on an ark when the world ends."

This was a game that could go on all day. "Christ, Victor, let's cut the shit. Marjorie and Noah are missing. I'm looking for them. If they're all right, that's as far as I'll go. Okay?"

He eyed me. He was thinking about it. "You doing this for money?"

"Yeah."

He nodded. That was okay. "Sonoma. She said something about going up to Sonoma, along the Russian River someplace. That's all I know. Maybe her grandma knows more."

"Her grandmother said she went to Tahoe."

"Maybe she did that, too. Or maybe I heard her wrong. I remember she said Sonoma. And that's all I know, and I got work to do."

"All right. Thanks."

"Any time, man." He turned away, dropped to the ground, and began to wriggle back under the car. He gave me one last look.

"Don't mess with Marjorie."

I walked away without answering. Mostly because I didn't know whether he was threatening me on his own account or warning me about the dangers of Marjorie, herself.

On my way back along the walkway, I passed the dogs. The puppies were tearing the stuffing out of a broken car seat. The adult dogs were asleep.

The woman was standing in the sun just outside the miniature door, which she had propped open with a corrosion-iced battery. We nodded politely to each other. She moved aside just enough to let me by. I looked back at her, once, as I was picking my way through the darkness of the office. She was watching me, so I didn't steal any bolts or anything on my way out.

THIRTEEN

I STILL HAD PLENTY of the day left, so I decided that, before I did any more work, I would take Carleton up on his invitation to visit the hat shop and look around. I found a parking place a block down from Telegraph on Dwight and strolled into the dim narrow shop for the second time in three days. I nodded to Carleton, who, busy with a customer, nodded back.

This time, I was looking at the merchandise. I ignored the rack of berets. After slouching around Berkeley-style for a few minutes, sneering at the overcrowded, ceiling-high shelves of headgear, I spotted a glass case, along one side, in which were perched about a dozen very beautiful fedoras. Soft felt in beige, brown, black, blue and forest green.

I approached the counter. "What do I have to do to try on one of those fedoras?" I asked.

"Just go around the back of the case and slide the door open." He looked pleased with me for some reason.

I did as he said. I found a brown one in my size and tried it on in front of a mirror that needed resilvering. Gorgeous. I was Alan Ladd. No, too tall. George Raft? Scott Brady? Thirty-five dollars. Not much for a great image. I wore it up to the counter.

"Mm-hm!" Carleton said admiringly. I grinned crookedly, film noir style, and paid the man.

"I guess you remember when guys wore those things the first time around, right, Jake?" He smiled innocently.

"I guess I should warn you," I said, smiling back, "that Victor's a little pissed off that you sent me over there."

"Yeah?" He laughed. "What's he gonna do, smear me with grease? Anything new on the case?"

"Hard to tell," I said cryptically, and headed for the door.

"Maybe the hat will help," he called after me. I did not turn back or answer him.

My car and my hat suited each other. First of all, there was none of that nonsense about headrests. People were tough in the fifties and didn't worry about things like broken necks. You can wear a hat in a 1953 Chevy. Modern cars, on the other hand, were built for an era of hatlessness. You cannot comfortably wear a hat, except a beret, in a modern car with a headrest. First of all, the ceilings are low. If you're even moderately tall, you'll smash your hat against the ceiling. If you slump to avoid this, or if you're short, you collide with the headrest. The back of the hat gets squashed, or the hat gets pushed down on your nose or off your head altogether.

I wonder what will happen if hats continue to be popular once again. Will cars change? Will hat racks and hatcheck concessions return to public places? I've seen people sticking their hats under their chairs in restaurants, sometimes forgetting them. Or stepping on them. And it's not much fun to wear a hat to go someplace when you have to take it off to drive there and back. The point of a hat is to wear it.

I, at least, in my headrestless classic, could drive down Telegraph wearing my new fedora. Sure, whiplash could be a problem. But me and my fedora and my '53 Bel Air, we didn't give a damn.

It wasn't easy to switch from my carefree mood to the chore I'd set for myself when I got home. It wasn't even

easy, I discovered, to find what I needed to begin the job
at all. After half an hour's search, though, I found it,
where it had slipped behind the astoundingly outdated
world atlas I had bought from a book club when I was
fourteen. The Old Testament. This, unlike the atlas, was
not a memento of my childhood. It was a souvenir of a
brief but uncomfortable relationship with an attractive,
odd woman who was trying to find herself by going back
to her roots: attending Friday night services, taking He-
brew classes, dating only Jewish men, that kind of thing.
The Bible had been a birthday present.

I hadn't worried much, at first, about the discrepancies
my father had pointed out in the construction of the ark.
After all, I reasoned, if a man decides he's the second
Noah, actually hears God saying so, he can decide damned
near anything else he wants—that the ark should be
smaller, that there should be two, three, or forty of them,
that God changed his or her mind about a promise that
was, after all, made a long time ago. A lot of water had
passed, so to speak, since the original flood.

But discrepancies are discrepancies.

I skimmed through the first five chapters of Genesis.
There he was, in Chapter 6, Noah himself. The original
one. I had only the vaguest memories of the text, from
Sunday school too many years before. But my strongest
memory—that the stuff was damned hard to follow—held
true.

Here was God talking about how evil man was, and
saying how he repented making such a wicked creature. So
he decided to destroy us, and, while he was at it, everything else—beasts, creeping things, and fowls of the air, it
said. Everything was corrupt. Except for Noah and his
family. So God told Noah to build the ark, and he told him
how to do it. Gopher wood and lots of pitch. I pulled out

my dictionary. Gopher wood. An unknown kind of wood, believed to be a kind of pine or fir. And there were the directions as to size: 300 cubits by fifty by thirty high. I looked up cubit. Sure enough, the dictionary, also, said it was the distance from the elbow to the tip of the middle finger. The Romans figured it at 17.4 inches, the English at a nice, round 18, and the Egyptians, who apparently had longer forearms than the others, at 20.6 inches. I thought I'd go with 18, an easy foot and a half. The ark was supposed to be three stories high, with a window and a door. Once it was built, God told Noah to hop aboard, and, while he was at it, take on two of every kind of creature and all kinds of food.

I remembered wondering, when I was a boy, how Noah was going to tell which of the animals were not corrupt. Or had God really meant that everything was corrupt? Or just people?

In Chapter 7 the issue was further confused. Now Noah was supposed to take the clean beasts on by sevens, the unclean by twos, and birds by sevens.

The Bible said Noah was six hundred years old. No wonder he was so good.

And then it rained.

Next came the part where it said "fifteen cubits upward did the waters prevail; and the mountains were covered." Wait a minute, I thought. I pulled out my nine-dollar solar-cell calculator. Fifteen times one and a half. The mountains had to be taller than twenty-two and a half feet. Were we all talking about the same cubits?

No wonder people have Bible study groups.

Chapter 9 was mostly about the no-more-floods covenant God made with Noah, to the effect—or so I gathered—that as long as humans were such bastards anyway, there wasn't much point in destroying the earth again when they acted like the bastards they were.

The next thing I couldn't figure out was this human superiority dominion stuff. Why would God give dominion over other creatures to someone whose imagination was "evil from his youth"?

As always, when I got involved in the poetic or the philosophical, I felt vaguely angry.

Then there was some stuff about requiring the blood of the man at the hand of every beast and at the hand of man, and the line about anyone who sheds man's blood getting his blood shed by man. Then Chapter 9 went on to a whole different subject, something about Noah being naked.

So there it was. I didn't know what to make of it. But my father was right. The ark was too small. Even if they had three or four of them. I slipped into a mathematical stupor, poking away at my calculator, trying to figure out how many of the smaller arks it would take to make the real thing. If a cubit really was eighteen inches, it would take at least fifty. Did they really have fifty of them? Were they lying to me? Was I going to spend the rest of the day multiplying any number of numbers by eighteen inches, coming up with wrong answers, building little three-dimensional drawings when numbers alone failed? I stowed my calculator and opened a light beer.

Tigris strolled in. "It seems to say here," I said, tapping the Bible, "that you're supposed to get a chance to kill a human, in return for being stuck under my evil thumb." She purred and jumped into my lap. "Heathen," I said. I gave her a couple of minutes under my thumb, then I gave her the whole chair and took a walk down to the corner.

About a dozen people were working. Arnold wasn't there, but Beatrice was, gamely hacking away at a two-by-four with a handsaw. Either she wasn't very strong or the saw wasn't very sharp. She was glad to stop and talk to me.

"I've been wondering about a couple of things," I began. "Maybe you could help me out."

She looked uncertain. We sat down on a stack of lumber.

"First of all," I said. "There's some confusion about Marjorie's disappearance. Her cousin Victor says he saw her before she left and she said something about Sonoma. Her grandmother says she called her on the Saturday and said she was on her way to Tahoe."

Beatrice wrinkled her nose, lifting her upper lip, a look of pain that, I guessed, meant distress of some kind.

"Gosh," she said. "I just don't know. See, she might have been going up to Sonoma, because she's gone there a few times, just to check things out and report back to Noah. I'm not sure she was supposed to go there that week. Usually, that's just between her and Noah. Although Arnold might know. But if that's what she told her cousin, then I suppose she was planning on going there. But you say she called Mrs. Burns?"

"And said she was on her way to Tahoe."

"Well, I just never heard anything about that."

"Could she have been going up to Noah's casino for any reason?"

"I suppose. As far as I know, she just worked on the arks, and didn't help him with other things, but . . ."

Not much help there, I decided, and went on to topic number two.

"About the arks," I said. "Noah's not exactly following the Bible in all this, is he?" I waved my hand, indicating the vessel and her workers. Beatrice looked vague, her face a Sandy Dennis smear of incomprehension. "The size. The size is wrong." Her features became more solid again.

"Yes," she said. "That's right. You mean the cubits. Three hundred by fifty by thirty."

"And three stories tall. This is one."

"Yes," she said. "The ark was really big."

"About cubits, now. The Bible says the flood went fifteen cubits upward. Are we talking about foot-and-a-half cubits here?"

"Of course. A cubit is eighteen inches." She was mildly interested. Here was a fact she knew.

"But it says the waters went fifteen cubits upward and the mountains were covered. That would make the mountains about twenty feet tall." How did I get into this, anyway?

She laughed, delighted little tinkles of laughter. I was very cute. "Oh, Jake. I don't know about your Bible, but mine says the water covered the mountains and then went fifteen cubits higher. Aren't you silly."

"I must have missed that." So it was settled. A cubit was a cubit.

"And how big is this ark?"

"It's one hundred cubits long by twenty-six wide by sixteen tall." A hundred and fifty feet by thirty-nine by twenty-four. "But of course," she added, "we have two of them. And our requirements are different."

I asked her how they were different.

"For one thing, we're not taking any animals. Just people. Carefully selected people." I allowed her the touch of smugness she showed just then, but it suddenly occurred to me that so far, no one had invited me. I put that aside for the moment.

"Right," I said, remembering that someone, maybe Beatrice, had mentioned that before. "You mean you're just going to let them all die?"

Her face smeared again. "You really should be talking to Arnold. Or even Noah. There's a really good reason."

"And that is?"

"God is going to take care of the animals. Because he promised never to destroy everything again, you see, and he doesn't trust us to do it right, anyway. We're being entrusted only with the selection of our own kind."

"I'm getting confused," I told her. "This is sounding less and less like the Bible story." I was, after all, an expert; I'd just read the thing that day, first time since about age nine.

"Oh, it's a lot the same."

"Maybe, but didn't God promise never to have another flood at all? He made a covenant with Noah."

"Oh, but you see...gee, I wish you'd talk to Arnold.... He did. But there were things in the covenant, other things. About capital punishment and animal rights. And we're not living up to those, so He wants to make a point."

Capital punishment. There was, indeed, something in that story about whoso sheddeth man's blood, about man shedding his blood right back again. Kill the killer, just as Arnold had said. But animal rights? I couldn't remember anything about that.

"We were given dominion over them," Beatrice explained. "And dominion implies responsibility. For instance, earlier in Genesis it specifically says God created the great whale. And look what we're doing."

Not noblesse oblige, I thought. Power oblige.

"It all has to do with victims, you see," Beatrice said brightly. "We just go around killing and destroying and nobody has to pay for it. We let killers go free and polluters, and..." she ran out of steam.

"So this flood is going to purge the planet of the people who make victims of everyone and everything else? And your carefully selected group believes in capital punishment and environmentalism and the rights of animals and other victims?"

She smiled. "Yes. But you should talk to Arnold. He knows more about it."

I didn't know whether I would or not. I thanked Beatrice and set out for home. Only in the eighties could such a collection of causes coalesce, I decided. The kind of person who cared about animals and the environment didn't use to be the kind of person who wanted criminals eliminated. Were Right and Left merging here into some weird hybrid? This eye-for-an-eye thing could get pretty dangerous if you mixed Old Testament justice with current-cause passion.

I thought of Marjorie. An angry young woman, justifiably so, who wanted so desperately for the world to be better that she had climbed off the dirty streets of reality and onto the deck of an ark.

Unless, of course, she'd seen the arks as a personal way out, and nothing more. And Noah. And his money. I preferred to think she'd tipped off into never-never land.

FOURTEEN

THE TOURISTS arrived at six. They had had, I could tell, a wonderful time. My father was laughing, Lee had a slight pink flush on her gorgeous cheeks, and Eva was chattering away about the seals on seal rock, which, I believe, are actually sea lions.

"So cute," she was saying. "Jake, is it true that killer whales eat them? I heard somebody say that."

I had some memory from some time back, something about somewhere up north.... "I guess so, I think I remember reading something in the paper. But I don't think it's a big problem."

"Not to you, maybe," she said indignantly.

"How did you like Chinatown?" I asked. My father was enthusiastic.

"Better than Chicago," he said. "Like you're in China. The smells, the shops, everybody talking Chinese. Wonderful." I'd taken him there once, on his first visit to the Coast, but we'd gone only for dinner. He had obviously loved his daylight tour. "Such interesting people," he added. "An ancient culture, a great civilization. Did you know a lot of Jews went there from Europe, to escape?"

No I hadn't, but I wasn't surprised. They'd gone to Argentina, too. Never any peace and quiet.

I turned to Eva. "And you? How did you like it?"

She shrugged. "I liked the seals."

"What about Chinatown?"

"Very interesting," she said. "Different. But I don't know..." I waited. "Who wants to look at old eggs and dead ducks?"

Lee laughed, and the angels sighed.

"Now," I said masterfully, "where does everyone want to go for dinner? What do you feel like eating?"

"Not Chinese," Eva declared. "Not today, anyway."

"Italian? Mexican? Japanese?" Lee asked.

"No raw fish," my father said.

"You don't have to eat raw fish in a Japanese restaurant," I told him.

"You know," Eva said, "I only had Mexican food once before. Interesting. Different. But good."

No one objected to that. I put on my fedora and took them to my favorite Mexican restaurant. I think, on the way, Lee glanced favorably at my hat.

The restaurant was just up the street, on College. For several years, this same place had specialized in authentic dishes native to the South Pacific. Now the same management had turned it into a mostly Mexican restaurant. The food was terrific, the service delightful, and they seemed to be having some success with their new menu.

We were seated by a young man who could have been anywhere from eighteen to twenty-five and who wore his dark hair short and spiky. I placed my hat carefully under my chair.

"Don't forget it there," my father warned.

"I won't."

The waitress was a member of the original, founding, Indonesian family. The cashier, who looked like Rudolph Valentino even unto the patent leather hair, was a new addition. The South Seas mural still covered one wall, but, on another wall, someone very skilled had painted a villa

set on a distinctly Mexican landscape, complete with se-
rape-clad inhabitants.

The clientele looked pretty much the same: Berkeley/
North Oakland young to middle-aged professional types
who probably owned pasta makers. The only difference
was, there were more of them than there used to be. Maybe
Guadalajara was just a catchier name than Oceania.

"Listen," my father said, "I'm paying, so you order
whatever you want." He studied the menu.

The waitress remembered me, although not by name.

"Good to see you again," she said.

I smiled my reply and checked out the beer list. They still
had Kirin, so that's what I ordered. My father asked for
red wine, but Eva decided that, having had wine once before that week, she'd had enough alcohol. Lee considered
a margarita, until she learned that they had only a beer and
wine license and made their margaritas with white wine.
She decided on the wine all by itself. The waitress went off
to get our drinks.

"So?" my father wanted to know, "what's good?"

I explained some of the items on the menu while Lee's
eyes wandered to Valentino. My father settled on a taco-
tamale combination. Eva went for the quesadillas, and I
was in the mood for chicken enchiladas verdes. Lee came
back from a dream long enough to order chili rellenos.

Okay, so I don't look like Valentino. More like James
Caan, I thought, with George Segal's nose. Curly dark
blond hair, some of it on my chest. Passionate lips. Strong
but sensitive hands. What more could she want? Besides
all that, I had maturity, which Valentino definitely did not
have. When she was forty, I thought, she'd probably be
chasing twenty-year-old tail. Women. They're all alike.

I chatted unconcernedly with Eva. Lee drifted back.

"Eva tells me you write articles, Jake, is that right?"

Hah. Just as I thought. Eva had talked about me to Lee, no matter what she said. I avoided my father's eye. I was afraid he would be either winking and smirking or looking elaborately secretive—or, worst of all, bearing my idiocy and impending death with courage and resignation. I wished they'd both go home to Chicago and leave me alone. With Lee. Who was probably wondering why I had not yet answered a perfectly ordinary ice-breaking question.

"Actually," I said, "I'm a kind of investigator."

"A kind of?" she repeated with interest.

I glanced around me at the nearby tables occupied by strangers.

"Maybe I can tell you more about it under more private circumstances."

Eva raised her eyebrows, probably in despair at the duplicity of the rutting male. I still did not look at my father. Lee appeared to be reserving judgment. A tough cookie.

Dramatic effect dictated a change of subject, veering away from my sinister self, so I asked her what she did for a living. It turned out she was an attorney, working for a small firm up in Santa Rosa. Our food arrived; I was hungry, which made me happy. I was still in control of my vital organs, despite Lee's presence. Nodding appreciatively at her choice of profession, I ate a few bites of enchilada. Good green sauce.

"Civil or criminal?" I asked, after a long swallow of beer.

"Criminal," she answered, sipping wine and not looking seductively at me over the rim of her glass. "But sometimes it gets pretty disgusting."

"Yes. I know what you mean."

"Do you really?" That flicker of interest again, almost flirtatious. What a killer.

I smiled at her, confident, tough. "I do. Really." The folks, trying their best to leave us alone, were carrying on a low-voiced conversation about their dinners.

Lee's eyes were no longer straying quite so often toward the cash register.

"Must be a tough field," I said. "Law, I mean. Overcrowded, isn't it?"

"It is. There must be almost as many attorneys in Northern California as there are psychotherapists." I laughed with her and felt a small flash of wonder. Was it coincidence, I asked myself, that I was so often attracted to women who were, in turn, attracted to overcrowded fields of work? Chloe was a journalist. Iris was a therapist. I decided that it wasn't. I liked women who were what they wanted to be, period.

"Were you always interested in law?"

"No. Are you familiar with Hammurabi?"

I had to think hard for a moment. It was a name, and he was dead. I knew that. Phoenician? Assyrian? No, wait a minute—Babylon. "The guy with the code of laws?"

"Right!" She was pleased with me. Very pleased. "I was an anthropology student. Got my bachelor's degree in cultural anthro. Archaeology. But I didn't know what to do with it. I had gotten interested in Hammurabi's code, realized maybe the law...." She shrugged. "Anyway, I came at it sideways."

"Archaeology," I said, eating some more enchilada. "I used to read a little ancient history now and then. You haven't been formally introduced to my cats, have you?"

She laughed. "Not formally, no. Why?"

"Their names are Tigris and Euphrates."

After that, I was sure she was giving me the edge over the cashier.

FIFTEEN

THE NEXT MORNING I got right down to business, calling Mrs. Noah to ask if it would be convenient for me to stop by. I wanted, I told her, to drop off some of the papers I'd taken from her husband's office.

"Did you learn anything from them?"

"Not much so far." That was true. I'd noticed that the man was rich, which I'd already figured out, and that he had indeed pledged the quarter of a million to the arks. I also learned that he'd been largely responsible for the funds that had gotten the arks started, as well. There were the lists of ark-people, but I thought I should go over those with Arnold at some point, to see if he could come up with anyone who might have been interested in doing the leader in. There was also a list, a very short list, of people who had donated various small sums to the construction: Beatrice, Arnold, and Joe Durell. I noticed that neither Jerry Pincus, Noah's Tahoe partner, nor Bert Olson, his mechanic, was on either list.

I kept the file of memos and notes, and some of the personal correspondence I hadn't had the time—or the inclination—to go through yet.

On my way over to the house, I saw an incredible-looking blond walking down Claremont Avenue, and, unavoidably, thought about the evening before. Lee had shaken my hand at the door and gone home to Petaluma—no surprise there—but she had held my hand a little longer than she'd needed to, and her smile had been a mite on the heavy-lidded side. We said we hoped we'd see each other again soon. I was planning to make sure of it.

I would find the time somehow.

I passed the Claremont Hotel and turned up the money-cushioned street. The big new American car was right where I'd seen it last, parked in front of the house on the movie-style driveway.

I pushed the bell. Adele, the maid, pulled the door open after a while and gazed at me sullenly. Her red hair, I reflected, was nothing like Lee's.

"Jake Samson," I said. "Mrs. Gerhart is expecting me."

She nodded, turned, and marched through the entry hall. I followed her, once again, to the library. June Gerhart was wearing a shirtwaist dress, heels, and a ribbon around her neck.

I put the folders down on a side table. She invited me to sit down.

"Is that everything?" she asked.

"No. I kept what I'm still using. I did want to talk to you about a few things, though."

She nodded. She was looking a little tired. New lines had appeared around her eyes since I'd seen her last.

"Are you having any success at all, Jake?"

"Yes, I think so. I'm following a lot of trails. I don't have the answer yet, if that's what you're asking, but I don't have all the pieces of the puzzle yet, either. I'm closing in on it."

I was no such thing. At that point, as far as I knew, I could keep following trails for the rest of my life and never find Noah or Marjorie or the quarter of a million. But I was certainly taking the case more seriously since my father had gotten bashed. Whatever was going on, it wasn't kosher.

"You said you had something you wanted to talk to me about?"

"Several things. One of the lists I found in your husband's papers had to do with investors. In the arks. There were only three: Arnold, Beatrice, and Joe. Each name had five thousand dollars written after it. Did they each give five thousand dollars?"

She shook her head. "I'm sorry, Jake, I just don't know. I don't know much about the finances for the arks. I had the impression that Joe had contributed something. He is involved, after all."

"I can't decide whether five thousand dollars is a lot of money or not very much, compared to what your husband was putting in."

"Oh, that sounds like a good amount. After all, the arks were Tom's project from the beginning. Other people gave what they could or what they thought would be suitable. Most people don't have a lot of extra money, you know."

"Are you saying Durell doesn't have much money? Doesn't he have an interest in Yellow Brick Farms?"

"Oh, yes. But Yellow Brick Farms is also primarily my husband's project. Joe has some shares—they'd be worth quite a lot now, I would think—and of course a generous salary."

"But he does have an interest. He shares in the profits, right?"

"That's right, in a small way."

"Well then, how does he feel about your husband's siphoning off profits from the company for the arks?" There was a logical answer to that: it was none of his business. But I had to ask.

"Oh, but that's not the way it works, Jake," she objected. "I think we need some sherry now, don't you?"

"Okay." I didn't need any, but if she did, what the hell. She picked up a little brass bell from the table beside her chair and tinkled it. Then she put it down again.

"Now, as I was saying, Tom was putting some of our share of the profits into the arks. He had every right to do that."

"But don't you have to plow a certain percentage, as they say, back into the business?"

"I believe," she said with finality, "that there is more than enough for both purposes. If Tom thinks so, it's so. He is a very good businessman. And Joe seems perfectly satisfied."

"Good. Good. I also wanted to ask you something about who's controlling the company."

She looked puzzled.

"Your husband's been missing for over a week now. Are you planning to take a more active part in the business, helping out, filling his shoes?"

She laughed lightly. "I don't think so. It hardly seems necessary. Of course, I've always been somewhat involved. I know some of the oldest, biggest customers, socially. I would certainly help if I were needed. But Joe has worked with Tom a long time. They've worked together so well, for so long, that I see no reason not to trust him to keep things going until Tom returns."

"I don't want to upset you or anything, but you do believe that your husband is at least in danger. What if he doesn't come back? Durell says you inherit his share of the business, is that right?"

"Of course."

"What would happen then? Would you take control of the company?"

She looked offended. "I'm not sure I know what you mean by control." She picked up the little bell and rang it again.

"I mean run the company. If you thought your husband wasn't coming back. Knew he wasn't." Did her lip tremble, or was I running a movie in my head?

"You mean move into my husband's office? Not unless I felt I needed to. If I heard of a problem of some sort...."

Her hesitation opened up another question. "Have you heard of any problems?"

"No, not really, just the kind of thing you might expect. You see, Joe lost his assistant a while ago, and there have been some minor tie-ups in deliveries. He just needs a little more help than he's got right now. Certainly, if Tom didn't come back, he'd need to do some hiring. But I don't think I would have to actually go out there and work. I wonder, would you excuse me for just a moment?" She left the room. I checked over my notes. Just a couple more items to go into with her, then I'd go back to the house, have some lunch with the folks, see if Rosie was home, and go on from there.

June came back with two glasses of sherry on a tray.

"Just a few more questions, okay?" She nodded, looking a lot more tired than she had when I'd first arrived. "Do you know someone who owns an old car? Dark blue. Early seventies. A dent in the side. A license number starting with C?" I described the mugger and the driver—not much in the way of descriptions, but something, anyway.

"How did you meet these people?"

"I'm not even sure they have anything to do with the case, June, but they might." I told her the big guy seemed to be looking for me.

She thought for a long time. Then she shook her head helplessly. "I'm sorry. I can't think who that could be."

"That's all right, it's just a long shot anyway. Don't worry about it. There's something else, something I've been wondering about for a while. It's about the ark. When they first started working on the one down on my corner, they were putting in reasonable workdays, not too long. But in the last couple of weeks they've been working constantly, putting in as many hours and days as they can without running into problems with the noise ordinance. Do you know any reason why they might have decided to speed up the work?"

She thought about that for a long time, too. "I do remember something about that. Tom mentioned something to me, it was right before he went away, I believe. Yes. Something about thinking the flood was going to come sooner. Or something. That's all I remember. Sorry."

"No, that's fine. I'll talk to Arnold about it. That's very helpful." She sipped a little more of her sherry, then put it aside. It had helped. Her color was better. "Just one more thing. I've got conflicting reports about Marjorie, or maybe they're not. I don't know. What I have is that she told someone she was going to Sonoma, and then told someone else she was going to Tahoe. I understand why she might be going to Sonoma. That was part of her job. Buy why Tahoe?"

"She said she was going to Tahoe? I don't understand that at all. I know she was doing work for Tom, but I thought it was only on the arks. I don't understand that."

I put my sherry aside, too, nearly untouched. "Could she have been doing other kinds of jobs, maybe connected with your casino?"

"We don't own the whole casino," she corrected me. "Just part of it. I don't know. So...she said she was going to Tahoe and Tom said he had her with him." For the first time, I saw a flicker of doubt about her husband.

"Does that worry you?" I asked. "Does that make you think he did just run off for some kind of fling?"

The doubt faded, replaced by anger. "No. Never. It had to be business."

I decided that I had spent enough time with her, shaken her more than enough. I said good-bye, told her I'd be in touch, and left her alone.

Rosie had told me she didn't think she'd be home before noon, and she wasn't. Or at least her truck wasn't, which was a pretty good indication. I passed right by the house and found a parking place near the copy shop on College Avenue. It took me half an hour to copy the pages in my notebook. Rosie was amazingly good at reading my handwriting, and those pages would give her a jumping off place on the case. She could run through them and then we could sit down for a couple of hours and go over the whole damned thing. If I was missing anything, she would be able to tell me what it was. While I copied, I planned out the rest of the day. Lunch. Then, if Rosie was back, a quick run over to Noah's mechanic's place. Maybe he knew something, maybe Noah had mentioned something to him. Maybe they were best pals. Who could tell? Then I wanted to spend some time going over what I had and trying to make some sense of some of it. And while I was doing that, Rosie could have a talk with Arnold—as good a way as any to get a hold on things—and ask him a couple of outstanding questions about the arks and their investors and passengers.

Then we were going to do some traveling. I didn't think Rosie would mind that too much.

SIXTEEN

EVA HAD MADE A BIG salad for lunch, with those tiny cooked shrimp in it. Just a few years ago she would probably have served something like beet borscht and blintzes, one with lots of sour cream mixed in, the other with lots of sour cream on top. My world has changed. We are dying of nutrition.

Rosie came back to find me just as we were finishing, said she'd eaten, and told me to come and get her when I was ready. The folks were just as friendly to her now as they had been before Lee had become a more likely prospect.

I told them that Rosie and I would probably be going out of town later that day on business. They thought that was a terrific idea, but much to my relief said they had plans. Which were? I asked. They were driving up to Petaluma and having dinner with Lee. Too bad, they said, I couldn't make it. They thought they might stay over, because Lee was taking some time off to give them a tour of the wine country the next day. Where would we be going?

"The Russian River, for starters," I said. "That's in Sonoma, too, but farther north."

Maybe they would join us there later the next day? I said we would be on our way to Tahoe, by then.

"Tahoe?" my father cried. "That's one of the places we want to be sure to go."

"I'm sorry, Pa, but we'll be working. And I don't really expect to stay there much more than overnight, either."

Maybe, he said, they would go on their own later in the week. Maybe Lee, he said, would go with them.

I escaped, and found Rosie sitting on her front deck reading a Robert Parker mystery. She stashed it next to her bed, told Alice it would be too hot for her to sit in the car, locked up the cottage with Alice inside, and followed me to my car.

Bert Olson's Auto Shop was down in West Berkeley, just off University Avenue. On the way there, I filled Rosie in on what I wanted her to talk about with Arnold, and asked her if there was any problem with going to the river that night.

She looked delighted, and said there shouldn't be any problem at all—she'd just need to find a dog-sitter.

Olson's shop was tucked away on an industrial side-street down the block from a lumberyard. It was a dirty white frame building with an office and garage space for three cars, two of which were filled. A sign over the garage doors said "We Specialize in Volvos and Other European Cars."

Olson was bending over the open hood of a Volkswagen Rabbit. I introduced myself and Rosie and asked if he could spare a few minutes to talk about a customer who had disappeared. He straightened up and turned a grease-smudged face to us, checking us out with something like disbelief. Amused disbelief.

He was a short, thin man dressed in filthy gray coveralls. Brown hair and a straggly reddish-brown mustache.

"And who might that be?" he wanted to know.

"A man named Tom Gerhart, owns a Volvo. A blue 1975 wagon."

He burst out laughing. "Disappeared, huh?"

"That's right," Rosie said. "Why is that funny?"

"Shit," he said, shaking his head. "What do you want to know about him?"

"You've been his mechanic for a long time, isn't that so?" she asked. He nodded, and wiped his hands on a greasy rag.

"I was just gonna take a break. Want a Coke?"

We followed him into his office, declining the drink. He got one for himself, from a machine just inside the door, hoisted himself butt first onto a paper-littered desk, narrowly missing a dangerous-looking spindle, and pointed at two plastic chairs in the corner. We sat.

The floor was vinyl tile, most of them gone or half-gone. But the office itself was reasonably clean, and looked as though it had been painted within the last half-decade or so. There was a bank of rickety, olive-drab file cabinets behind the desk.

"Now, to answer your question," he said, "I have been Tom Gerhart's mechanic for a long time, yeah."

"So you must know him fairly well?" I asked.

He grinned. "Well enough. Not like we was brothers or anything."

"So," I continued, "why do you think it's funny that he's disappeared?"

"Why don't you tell me a little something about this disappearance?"

I told him. "Do you think it's likely he would have run off with a woman?" I asked. "Did he maybe mention anything about having some problems or having to go somewhere?"

He took a long drink from the Coke can. "Can't say about the woman. He never said nothing about women at all. Never even a good, dirty joke. As to problems, well, that goes without saying, don't it?"

"What do you mean?" Rosie asked.

"Well, shit, girl—'scuse me, I should say woman, I guess"—he winked at her—"the man is crazier 'n a fuckin' bedbug. I would call that a problem of sorts, wouldn't you?"

"What makes you say that?" I felt like an idiot asking the question, and the man looked at me like I was one, for sure.

"A man thinks he's Noah? A man builds an ark because the flood is coming? Shit." He laughed again. "Don't get me wrong, I like old Tom. Nice guy, good customer. But fuckin' apeshit, man. I told him so myself, when he asked me did I want a spot in the ark. I told him, 'Tom, you're fuckin' nuts.' Of course I kind of thought so before that, anyhow."

"Oh, yeah?" Rosie grabbed hold. "Why is that?"

He shook his head again, and looked from one to the other of us like an uncle talking to a pair of not-too-bright kids. "The guy's got millions, you know? You ever seen his house?" I nodded. "Shit. Millions. And he was driving a 1975 car?" He laughed again, snorting a little. "Don't get me wrong. That's a good car. But millions, man. And he's driving a ten-year-old station wagon."

"There's nothing wrong with liking old cars," I said.

"Old-old, yeah, maybe. But middle-aged?" His wit cracked him up again. "Over and over I told him, 'Tom, you're fuckin' nuts.'"

"Now that we've established that," Rosie said, smiling a little despite herself, "when did you last see him?"

He closed his eyes to think. "About a month ago. Had her in for an oil change. Never lets it even begin to get dirty. But I heard from him about a week ago. He called me long-distance. On a Sunday."

"What Sunday? And from where?"

He slid off the desk and went around it to look at his calendar. "Must of been the fifteenth. Yeah, Sunday the fifteenth." The day after he'd left the note for his wife.

"From where?" Rosie repeated.

"From Tahoe. Said he was having some vapor lock problems and wanted to know if I knew a good mechanic up there. You know, at that altitude—"

"Yeah," I said. "Did he say anything else?"

"Not that I remember. I don't know anyone up there, so I couldn't help him out. He said thanks anyway and good-bye."

That was all he had. It did not exactly sound like a message from a kidnapped man.

"If you hear from him again," I said, "would you let me know?"

Olson looked doubtful. "I don't know about that, man. Maybe the guy doesn't want to be found. Even crazy people got rights. That's what Berkeley's all about." He burst out laughing again.

"He may be in trouble," Rosie said. "Maybe if you hear from him you could tell him we're looking for him? We just want to be sure he and this Marjorie are all right."

He plunked himself down in a plastic upholstered swivel chair that looked like Jack the Ripper had had a go at it, and poured the rest of his drink down his throat.

"Sure. I could tell him that." I gave him my phone number and thanked him for his help. He followed us out of the office and returned to the gaping Volkswagen. He was chuckling happily to himself.

When we got home, I ran down to Rosie what I wanted to ask Arnold, handed her a couple of files from Noah's desk, walked her down to the corner, performed introductions, and left her there, returning to my house. I set myself up in a lawn chair with the rest of the files and my notebook, some paper, and a couple of sharpened pencils.

An hour or so later, Rosie and Alice walked up the path. Rosie pulled up another lawn chair and sighed deeply.

"Did you have fun?" I asked.

"Yeah. I'm such a great talker. I really love sitting around with middle management and trying to cut through the bullshit. Anything interesting in what you've been reading?"

I closed the file folder I was holding. "Nothing that seems very important. The personal stuff includes some memos from Arnold about lumber and tools. There's some plans, drawings of the ark. A letter from some employee over at Yellow Brick Farms complaining about being fired. Lots of lumber receipts—do you think he plans to deduct the arks from his income tax?—but not a damned thing that might lead us to someone who might want to get Noah for any reason."

"What about the fired employee?"

"Fired by Durell."

"Oh."

"Anyway, if we're looking for some guy who just wanted a quarter of a million, just an ordinary, everyday violent thief, I haven't found any leads to him. How about you?"

"I went over the lists with Arnold. He didn't know of any other contributors—pardon me, investors. See, most of the people on that membership list aren't putting up any money at all. Arnold says all Noah required for a place on the ark was a certain amount of labor. Quite a lot of labor. And more lately."

"About that—you asked him why they've been speeding things up?"

"Sure. Not much help there, though, either. Arnold says Noah told him he'd 'gotten word' that the flood might be coming sooner than they thought."

"When did he get this word?" Euphrates jumped into my lap, a large ball of lead, purred for a while, and fell asleep.

"A few days before he disappeared. Arnold says he asked Noah if he'd had another dream, and he said he hadn't."

"I feel like that should be significant somehow, but I can't see where it fits."

"Not yet, anyway. But I'm way behind you on this."

"We're going to fix that today."

"Good. I also took a tour of the ark. Interesting. I've never seen a ship being built before, so I can't tell whether it'll float or not. Anyway, I talked to Arnold a little about the differences between the original ark and this one, and he said they didn't need as much room because—"

"God was going to take care of the animals?"

"Right. I think Noah's pretty good at making his visions suit practical necessity."

"Yeah. He's not as crazy as Bert Olson thinks he is."

She laughed. "I don't think the modifications are particularly significant, do you?"

"No. And it's too bad. I spent all that time reading the Bible. You ready to throw yourself completely into this case?"

"Sure. What's next?"

"We need to do some traveling. First, I thought we'd run up to the Russian River and have a look at the ark up there, talk to some people, see if Marjorie was up there and when. Then, from there—Tahoe. I'll bet we can even manage to have some fun while we're working.''

Rosie had no objections. The river and Tahoe are two of her favorite places.

SEVENTEEN

I'VE ALWAYS LIKED the Russian River, too. A small river, broad and shallow, coming down out of the north and sweeping through Sonoma County, through the redwoods and the rolling coastal hills, a slow and gentle current to the ocean.

The River, a resort area of considerable beauty and strange inconsistencies, is beaded with tiny towns from up around Cloverdale to Jenner-by-the-Sea, known to the mapmakers as Jenner. Most of these tiny towns don't qualify as towns at all, but as "communities" of fewer than 250 souls. Little stopping places. A store. A gas station. A place to rent a canoe. A motel. The chief industry is tourism.

Inconsistencies? Here's a knockout of a resort country, less than two hours from the metropolitan Bay Area, with nice, if rocky beaches, a river even a moron couldn't drown in, lodges, inns and resorts ranging from rustic to elegant, and great food. And the smell of rural poverty. Plenty of real estate available at a good price. But the only jobs in any number are connected with tourism, unless you commute to Santa Rosa, which is a big town but not exactly Detroit. I had a friend once who bought a beautiful house right on the river and didn't make it through the first winter.

"Jesus, Jake," he said, "it's damp and dark and deserted. And depressed. And too far away." He moved to a condo in Napa.

I guess people are just never satisfied. I don't think it's any damper up there than in, say Mill Valley or the Berkeley Hills.

Anyway, I like it, and I was glad to get a chance to drive up there, stay overnight, hit a couple of restaurants, paddle a canoe, and go on, lungs refreshed, with possibly a little more information about Noah's disappearance than I had when I left home.

Before we left, I called Rico and asked him to look after the cats until I got back or my folks returned from their visit with Lee. He told me my father was a fine man. I agreed. We dropped Alice off with a dog-owning friend and headed north.

When we passed through Petaluma I thought of calling Lee, but there wasn't much point in it, since I was going to be pretty busy for the next few days. We were on our way to Guerneville, one of the main towns on the river, and planned on getting there in time for an early dinner at the Bugle, a very big resort with dozens of cabins, a campground, a classy restaurant, a good bar, a pool, river frontage, and canoes. It also happens to be a gay resort, but the rest of the locals, as far as I know, aren't complaining. It brings a whole lot of business into town.

I drove through the jammed parking lot once, gave up, and left the Chevy across the road. We got a couple of tequila sunrises at the bar and took them outside to a table overlooking the pool. It was close to six p.m. but still warm, and there were half a dozen men and two women swimming. The ratio in the bar was about ten to one, men leading. I asked Rosie about the preponderance of men.

"They own the place," she shrugged. "Their brochures and advertising are aimed at men. And the men tend to have a lot more disposable income to spend on fancy resorts."

I decided not to think about that. Instead, I suggested
dinner, since there wouldn't be much daylight after seven-
thirty or so, and we wanted to try to catch the people at the
ark that evening. Like the Oakland crew, they were probably working late.

The scampi was good, but a little too buttery for my
taste or my waistline. It would have been nice to take a
walk, but that would have to wait. We drove to a small
motel down the road, checked in, and headed for the ark.

According to Arnold's directions, the ark was sitting on
a lot tucked back in the woods about five miles from
Guerneville. We followed the River Road west behind a
metallic blue 1950 Hudson Hornet sporting a bumper
sticker that said, "Santa Rosa, Keep Your Shit to Yourself." This was in reference to the time the overgrown
town, having failed to keep its sewage facilities up to its
contractors' wildest fulfilled dreams, had filled all its
holding tanks to capacity and then dumped the overflow
into the river—a river that provides both recreation and
drinking water for all the communities downstream.

This act of vandalism was followed by a lot of hearings
and moratoriums and the like, which may force the city of
Santa Rosa to contrive, by foresight, to keep it to itself.

The river was visible through the trees on our left most
of the way to Monte Rio, population 1,150, four miles
along, which has less of a carnival atmosphere than
Guerneville, despite the banner across the road that says,
"Welcome to Monte Rio, Vacation Wonderland."

Our directions took us one mile west of the Vacation
Wonderland, more or less, where we were supposed to spot
a dirt road winding off to our left.

We did. It led through tall, dank redwoods and narrowed to a car's width after the first fifty yards. A quarter
of a mile or so into the woods, in the middle of a cleared

lot fringed with trees and ferns, we found the ark. The setting was shady and dark in the early evening, maybe even dismal. No one was singing.

The ark looked to be at about the same stage of construction as the one in Oakland. Work lights clamped to poles, running off the same kind of portable generator. Half a dozen people hammering and sawing. One of them came to meet us as we stepped down out of the car.

"Can I help you?" The pretty teeth he flashed at us contrasted nicely with his tanned face. I wondered where he'd gotten the tan; not here.

Rosie and I told him who we were, and that we were friends of Arnold's, just having a look around. He ran his fingers through his yellow hair. "We're kind of busy," he said, "but let me just tell Joe you're here." He headed toward the ark and we followed him, up the ladder onto the scaffolding and up onto the deck. He looked a little persecuted by our pursuit, but I didn't much care. There was an open hatch on the deck. We all went through it down to the hold.

The few portholes didn't do much to light up the huge, nearly bare interior, since nothing was coming in but filtered early evening gray. A couple of worklights were hooked onto the ribs near a large table flanked by two chairs. A man was sweeping the floor, or whatever the bottom of the boat is called. He looked up. It was a Joe I knew, Joe Durell. He dropped his broom in the pile of sawdust he'd made and strode over, smiling, to greet us. He looked as tired as he had the last time I'd seen him.

"Jake! How you doing? What can we do for you?" The young man who had inadvertently brought us down there sighed audibly. Everything was okay. I was a good guy.

"This is my partner, Rosie Vicente," I said. "Rosie, Joe Durell of Yellow Brick Farms."

"Great," Durell said. "Glad to meet you. I was just going to go up for some air. Come on." He grabbed my elbow and guided me back to the ladder and up to the deck. He didn't touch Rosie, but she trailed along anyway.

There were a couple of wooden crates and the inevitable pile of lumber up top. We sat.

"Do you come up here a lot?" Rosie asked.

"Quite a bit," he said. "When I'm not running Yellow Brick, I'm keeping an eye on things here."

"Keeping an eye on?" I asked. "You mean you're running this project?"

"Hell no, Jake, I just don't have that kind of time. Fred—that young fellow who brought you down to see me—he does the day-to-day management."

"Then maybe we need to talk to him, too," I said. "We think Marjorie might have come up here sometime during the week before she and Noah disappeared. We'd like to know exactly when that was—if it happened at all—and who saw her and talked to her."

He nodded thoughtfully. "Don't see why that should be a problem. What exactly was it you heard? Did anybody get more specific than 'sometime during the week?'"

"Not sure. When was the last time you saw her?"

"Oh, Jesus, Samson. Let's see. I think it was early last month some time. I was down in Oakland on business, stopped by the ark."

"You didn't see her up here, at this ark?"

"She's only been up here a couple of times that I know of. Once in August—I talked to her then—and I heard she stopped by here just a couple weeks ago. But I wasn't here and I don't remember when it was. We sure can do some asking around, though."

"We'd appreciate that," Rosie told him. He bobbed to his feet. He climbed most of the way down the ladder and hopped lightly to the ground. Not bad for a guy past forty-five. I was right behind him, and I didn't even hear his knees crack. He raised his hand at the guy with the teeth, who came right over.

"Fred," he said, "these folks want to know when was the last time Marjorie Burns came around. Jake here says he heard she stopped by. When would that have been, Jake, the week of the ninth?" I nodded.

"Probably," I said, "the end of the week. Possibly Saturday morning."

Fred ruminated, scratched his blond head. "I do remember seeing her, but I can't be sure when it was. I wouldn't have written it down or anything…the end of the week? That sounds about right. That's a week ago." He turned suddenly to Durell. "That would have been right before they left, her and Noah, right?"

"That's right. You don't remember what day it was, do you?"

He shrugged. "Damn, I really don't. Let me go ask a few people if they remember." He trotted off.

"I should explain something to you," Durell said. "Not everyone working on the arks knows that Noah actually disappeared. Some of the key people know, of course, like Fred, but we didn't want to upset people until we absolutely had to. That's why he said 'left.' Not vanished. A careful way we've gotten into the habit of talking."

"Probably a good idea," I said absently, watching Fred collar one worker after another.

He came back. "No one remembers what day it was. It wasn't a big event or anything. She stopped by from time to time, so she could tell Noah we were on schedule, I guess."

"You know that she and Noah disappeared, right?" Rosie asked.

"Yes."

"What do you think happened to them?"

He glanced at Durell, who said, "Go ahead, Fred. You can tell these people what you think."

"I don't know what to think. I know that some of the people who know Noah best think there's something wrong. But I guess I don't want to believe that. As for Marjorie, she seemed okay, pretty much the same as usual. I guess the point is we have to keep up people's spirits, and their belief that he wouldn't abandon them."

"You sound like you think maybe he did just take off," Rosie said.

"Heck no. I never said that. And I don't believe it. We're really pretty busy. Is that all you wanted from me?"

"For now," I said.

With some difficulty, I swung the car around and got it back on the road.

"Not terrifically helpful," I commented.

"No," Rosie agreed. "Kind of a weird spot, isn't it?"

"No weirder than a street corner in Oakland."

We decided to take in a little night life before we turned in.

The place we chose was big and noisy and had lots of rooms and lots of people dancing. It was outside of Guerneville, along the road to Santa Rosa, and Rosie had been there before. None of the women so much as glanced at me. A couple of the men did, briefly. Rosie ran into some people she knew, but mostly she danced with me, since no one else would. We danced until we were dizzy, drank modest quantities of beer, and then, since we were not in love with each other, got tired and went back to our motel. It was an early night.

Next morning, also early, we had pancakes at a place which was, according to a sign in the window and several proclamations on the menu, famous for its pancakes. They were good. So good that we decided we'd better take a little stroll to work them off.

We walked to the far end of the main street, taking in the atmosphere. A combination of Old West and new tourism. A little cute, maybe, but pleasant and cheerful. A bunch of restaurants, all of which looked good. Friendly people. Rosie was wearing her Gertrude Stein tee shirt, which collected some smiles. Male couples, female couples, mixed couples. Rosie in her tee shirt and macho me. Then we turned around and walked back to the motel.

The day before, I'd noticed a sign on the office wall that said CANOES FOR RENT.

It was a beautiful morning, warm and sunny, and not yet ten o'clock. We were self-employed, and that has to be worth something. I suggested an hour in a canoe before we checked out and left for Tahoe. Rosie agreed happily. We paid what seemed to me to be a small deposit—$15—for a padlock key and went out back to unchain our canoe.

The motel backed up onto the river, so we didn't have to carry the thing very far. We man- and woman-handled it down a steep bank, and set off downstream to explore.

You don't have to work very hard to canoe the Russian River upstream, and you don't have to work at all to go downstream. It carries you along, slowly, in its current. What you do have to do, though, is watch out for submerged branches, and keep an eye on the bottom. It is possible to run aground twenty feet from shore. Running aground presents no dangers. Neither, for that matter, does capsizing. But drifting is nicer. We drifted. We didn't talk.

The river is at its shallowest in the fall, before the rains start again, many months after the last rain of the winter before. There was just enough to swim in, and we slid past a few swimmers. The water was warm. The bottom was rocky enough to bruise the feet. Occasionally, Rosie would get a sudden urge to exercise and would paddle strenuously for a bit, and I, at the stern, would go along with the gag and work at steering.

We ran into the bank a few times, bumped the bottom, hit some rocks, but mostly managed to keep our aluminum craft in the narrow channel where the water was more than a couple of feet deep. The number of houses visible near the bank dwindled outside of Guerneville, but occasional dwellings showed above the trees. Houses with high decks built for the view.

Going back upstream, we paddled hard enough to get back before the hour was up.

I felt a little sad when we checked out. My own bedroom, my own bathroom. I could walk ten steps through that motel room without falling over a suitcase or a pot roast or a bowl of soup.

EIGHTEEN

BY ELEVEN O'CLOCK we were on our way east to the Sierras, and feeling good, looking forward to spending some time in Tahoe.

Not that either of us is a heavy-duty gambler. The best I've ever done is break even for the trip, which isn't bad. But that only happened once. Usually I dump a hundred or so, write it off—to myself, not to the IRS—as entertainment, and go home.

Rosie had skimmed through my notes on the way to the river, and she was reading them now. I don't know how she does that. I can't read in a car without getting sick.

She asked me a few questions, and I gave her some of my impressions of the people in the case she hadn't met, which was nearly everybody.

"You think this Carleton guy's okay?" she asked.

"I like him, but that doesn't mean he's okay. I think he could be a hothead under the right circumstances."

"And getting dumped can be just the right circumstances."

We had no disagreement there.

The Chevy is not air-conditioned, and neither is the California Central Valley. We drove with all the windows open, watching miles of dusty farmland, flat as anywhere in the Midwest, slip by, stopping for a quick and tasteless lunch at a place outside of Sacramento. The weak iced tea tasted great.

Our first sight of the Sierras ahead was like a mirage in the desert.

We came up over Echo Summit in midafternoon, the lake below us shining like a blue gemstone set in a ring of mountains.

Tahoe is the classiest of the gambling towns, for my money. Which is why classy Northern Californians and their money go there. Rosie, who had driven the last half of the trip, spotted a vacancy sign at a small motel two blocks from the main street and pulled into the parking lot. We lucked out on adjoining rooms, tossed our bags inside, and drove to a casino in the middle of town to get ourselves a beer and lay out our line of attack. We strolled virtuously through the banks of singing slots to the bar. But the poker machines set into the bartop were irresistible. I bought some dollars.

"Jake," Rosie said, "those are dollars."

"I know. Ten of them. Here, have a couple."

"A couple?" I handed her five.

First one in the slot got me the eight, nine, ten, jack of hearts, and the jack of clubs. Sadistic bastards. A pair of jacks pays even money. I went for the straight flush and got a six of spades. One dollar down. I drank some beer and dropped another one in the hole. Bells were ringing over in the quarter slots somewhere. But not for me. The computer dealt me a pair of eights, spades and clubs, and an assorted four-five-six. Big decision to be made here. The eights were worthless. There's no payoff on anything lower than jacks. The alternatives were to try for three—or even four—of a kind, or, possibly, a second pair, or try for the inside straight. I tossed in the four, five, and six and drew a four, a five, and a seven.

Rosie wasn't doing much better than I was. She'd gotten a high pair, two pairs, and a hand that was great for low-ball but not for anything else.

Then I stuck with a pair of jacks and got another one on the draw.

No more luck after that, which was probably a good thing, since we did have work to do. We lost the last couple of dollars, got a couple of city maps, marked out our territories, and set off, me in the car, Rosie in a cab, to interview garage mechanics. I'd had copies made of the photos of Marjorie and Noah, and we each had a set. We would meet back at the motel at seven, have dinner and compare notes.

I slogged around until 6:45, talking to service station attendants and auto mechanics, flashing my photos, describing Noah's car. I met a lot of people. I even bought some gas. Nobody remembered seeing either the car or the people.

I went back to the motel and put in a call to my answering machine to see if anything was happening back in Oakland. There were two messages. Lee wanted me to call her when I got back. Arnold wanted me to call him immediately. Very important, he said, and his voice sounded a little hysterical. I called the number he'd left on the tape. No answer. Then I took a long shower and stretched out. I was hoping Rosie'd had better luck than I'd had.

She showed up about ten minutes later, and she had some news. She'd found the place where Noah's car had been worked on. The mechanic remembered Marjorie, remembered the car. He was pretty sure she'd come in alone. He looked up the work order—it was for Monday the sixteenth—and found the motel name Marjorie had given him as an address and the phony name she'd given for herself. Beatrice Hinks.

I told Rosie about the message from Arnold.

"He sounded upset?"

I shrugged. "He's such a nervous little guy, it's hard to tell. But yeah, I'd say he was upset about something. Could be just because I took off without telling him. Who knows? How hungry are you?"

"I could wait a while."

"Let's, then. I'd like to go check out Pincus and the casino."

"What about the motel Marjorie gave as her address?"

"That, too, or maybe dinner and then the motel."

Mrs. Noah had told me the casino was called Jerry's Jackpot. Information gave me the number, the employee who answered the phone told me where it was. A half-mile or so down the road from the biggest cluster of Tahoe business.

It wasn't the smallest casino in town, it was maybe the second or third smallest. Noah was, or had been, a rich man. But ordinary multimillionaire wealth was not, apparently, enough to buy a piece of a really big palace of dreams.

No one was standing outside passing out coupons for free dollars, but the lack of come-on didn't seem to be hurting business any. The place had a lot of slot machines and I didn't see many that weren't being fed. There was a nice little bar in the far corner, the road to which was lined with nickel and dime slots. You couldn't get near the poker, twenty-one, or roulette without being tempted to drop some spare change into the bread-and-butter fund. Once you did get past the slots, though, you could see that the place was one big room. Only the poker players were segregated, behind an Old West-style banister that partitioned off a couple of tables at the left-hand side of the room. At the back were one roulette table, three twenty-one games, and three craps tables.

I asked the cashier where I could find Jerry Pincus. She told us he was in his office upstairs. She didn't ask if we had an appointment. She'd probably put a lot of energy into not becoming someone's "girl Friday," and she wasn't about to blow it by acting like one now.

The second floor of Jerry's had a lot more slots, a bingo game, and keno. There were a couple of change people, a woman and a man, running around with their little coin belts. I stopped the guy and asked him where I could find Pincus's office.

"I don't know if he's there," he said. "Is he expecting you?"

"Yeah," I lied. He glanced toward the back wall, pointing with his chin. I could see a small added-on cubicle back there, with a sign on the door that I figured probably said PRIVATE. It did. I knocked.

A deep, soft voice on the other side wanted to know who was there. I told him, adding that we wanted to talk about his business partner, Thomas Gerhart, that we were working with Arnold Wolfe.

There was a brief silence. Then, "Come in."

I pushed open the door and entered a very small cubicle, with a desk directly across from the door and a four-drawer file cabinet to the right of the desk. The man in the swivel chair was facing the door across the desk. He stood up, leaned over the littered surface, grabbed my hand, let it go, smiled at Rosie, jerked a thumb at a couple of straight chairs on our side of the desk, and sat down again. We sat, too.

Neither the office nor the man suited my image of what a gambling casino owner and his surroundings should look like. The office was utilitarian; he worked there. Pincus was a very tall, very thin man. He should have been short and fat, flashily dressed, and sweaty, with thinning, or thinned, greasy hair. There should have been a sleazy blond lounging in a corner.

That's one of the problems with approaching middle age—I plan to approach middle age, warily, until I'm at least sixty-five—it's like you turn some kind of corner and too many things aren't what you expected them to be.

Anyway, he was very tall and very thin, with healthy hazel eyes, lots of sandy hair, and freckles on his face and arms. He was wearing a yellow shirt with an alligator on it and white cotton pants. He was about my age.

"Okay," he said, "what about Tom?"

"I assume you've heard that he's disappeared?"

He stared at me. "What's that mean?"

"It means that nobody seems to know where he is. Unless you do."

He raised his hands helplessly. "Tell me more." This man was good at saying nothing and getting someone else to dump everything he knows.

I told him about the dear June letter. He shook his head.

"Hard to tell what that might mean."

"What about Marjorie?" Rosie asked. "Do you know anything about any relationship he might have with her?"

"Even if I did, and I don't, that's not the kind of thing I'd involve myself in." He softened his answer, smiling at Rosie again. This was, undoubtedly, supposed to make us veer off. It didn't work. I can't stand self-righteous twerps who claim to have no normal curiosity.

"Have you ever met Marjorie?" Rosie asked. He was silent for a moment. Then he decided to own up.

"Sure. She did some work for Tom from time to time. Good businesswoman."

"She was up here recently," I said. "What do you know about that?"

"Recently? When would that have been?"

I told him.

He flipped back some pages on his desk calendar. I wanted to scrape the freckles off his face.

"Yes," he said finally. "She was here."

Through clenched jaws, I said, "Why don't you tell me about it?"

He shrugged. "She was here. To see me." He leaned back in his chair a little, and with every appearance of frankness and innocence, he added, "Business."

"What kind of business?"

He looked irritated. "Just business . . . Samson, is it?"

"Secret business?"

"None-of-your-business business."

Rosie stepped in. "Was she by herself, or was Gerhart with her?"

"She was alone."

"What day was that?"

He glanced again at his calendar. "Sunday the fifteenth, I believe." That was the day Noah's mechanic said he'd called him from Tahoe.

"You sure you didn't see Gerhart?"

"I didn't see him." It was my turn to gaze at him, but his eyes didn't waver.

"How did she seem?" I asked.

"You mean, did she seem like a woman who had just run off with her lover?" I didn't answer. "She seemed like a woman who was up here to take care of some business of her employer."

"Did she say anything about when she was returning to the Bay Area, or if she was returning, or if she was on her way somewhere else, or where she last saw Gerhart, or when?"

He looked slightly amused at my irritation. "No."

"Did she say where she was staying?"

He looked me firmly in the eye. "No."

"You were in business together," Rosie said, "but now he's disappeared. Where does that leave you?"

He thought about it. "I don't know that he's really disappeared, do I?"

"No, he could be dead." Rosie suggested.

Pincus looked at her, shocked. "That wasn't what I meant. Maybe he has run off for some reason, but I'll hear from him sooner or later."

"What if you don't?" I barked.

He smiled sweetly and shrugged.

"What kind of agreement do you have about his shares? If he's dead, who gets them?"

"His wife." He sat forward in his chair, elbows on desk, chin on interlocked fingers, and looked first at Rosie, then at me. "Are you trying to get at something?"

"Yes," I told him. "I'm trying to find out if you had any reason to kill the man."

He looked perplexed. "Who said anything about killing?"

"Or," I continued, "if you had any need for the money that seems to have disappeared with him."

He looked interested. "How much money was that?" I told him. He laughed. "I don't know anyone who doesn't have a need for a quarter of a million dollars."

"But maybe you have a particular need for it. Business problems?"

"Hell no. This is a good business. Maybe you noticed on your way up here."

"Why won't you talk about what Marjorie was doing here, Pincus," I shot back at him. "What are you hiding?"

He stood up. First he spoke to Rosie. "Excuse me," he said. Then he turned to me. "I don't know who you are, Samson, and I don't know what you're doing here—"

"I told you. We're working for Arnold Wolfe and we're looking for—"

"—And I don't care what your story is. I'd like to see you get your ass out of my office. But feel free to come back anytime you want that ass whipped."

"I hope you're including me in that threat," Rosie said. He ignored her, and continued to stare at me.

There are several ways to deal with threats. I decided to back off for the moment with one of my own.

Graciously, smiling a dangerous smile, I told him. "We'll be around, and we'll be back. You shouldn't have threatened me, Pincus. Now I'm pissed off."

Rosie and I stood up, cool.

"I'm sorry to hear you're coming back," he said, taking his seat again. "I wouldn't recommend it. But I'll be here all evening." He smiled. I smiled. We left.

"Really gets the old adrenaline going, doesn't it, Rosie? I bet it's going to be a good ten minutes before I can choke down my dinner."

"I'll need fifteen."

We decided against the eat-all-you-want casino buffets. They're a great buy if you can stuff yourself until you're sick and not eat for two days afterward. But that doesn't work for me. If I eat too much at night I just want to eat too much in the morning. We went to a place I knew. Continental. It had been two years, but the restaurant looked and smelled the same. Rosie opened with escargot, I ordered blue points. I used to like escargot, back when I lived in the Midwest and had never met a living snail. I just don't feel the same about them any more.

Rosie took a walk to the ladies'. I thought about Jerry Pincus. I remembered guys like him from high school. They never had names like Jacob or Marvin. They were often named Jerry. I gave this Jerry a probable life story. His father owned a car dealership. The family had a big house in a prewar section of a close-in suburb. He probably had a younger sister who worshipped him and fell in love with his friends. He played basketball. He wasn't particularly witty or intelligent or terrific-looking, but the teenage girls who were closest to their instincts liked him a lot. It had to do with survival and reproduction. They knew he would do well in the world they understood. He seemed to know about money and psyching out the other guy and when to make a move and when to slip sideways and when to take a chance and when to dig in. He knew about those things in the same way that some people understand color and form and design.

And because he was close to his instincts in the same way those girls were, he would choose one of them: beautiful, bright enough to raise the children but not bright enough to get bored with him and their life. She would create a home and enhance his prestige. He would create money and security and maybe even a dynasty. These people find each other, and neither one is ever tempted to wander off in search of self, or truth, or anything else. They seem to be born with the practical wisdom that never leads to adventure or art, or the real, ugly danger of life on the outside.

Oh, sure, occasionally a Jerry will make a mistake. He'll marry someone with flawed genes who, after a decade or so, starts drinking or screwing around. Or he'll get caught cheating on his income taxes.

But those are the exceptions. Most Jerrys lead safe, satisfied lives. More power to them, I suppose. Am I jealous? Probably.

Rosie came back. The rest of dinner arrived, her tournedos and my trout.

"What do you think, Jake? Did he see Noah? Did he know he was up here?"

"Maybe. Then again, maybe Noah didn't want Pincus to know he was in town for some reason."

"Why would he do that? Because he was having an affair with Marjorie?"

I shook my head. That wasn't it. "No. I think Pincus could be trusted with that information. Like he said, it's not the kind of thing he involves himself in."

"I don't like him. I think he could kill someone."

"I don't know." I told her about the Jerrys.

"That's ridiculous," she laughed. "The man owns a casino, for God's sake. Is that the kind of thing a Jerry would do?"

"Sure. It's not so different from running a car dealership, and probably more profitable."

She looked doubtful. "I guess. But how would I know? I grew up with grapes. I didn't know any Jerrys."

We rejected the dessert cart and found our next stop on the map. The Bon Chance Motel.

NINETEEN

IT LOOKED LIKE most of the other small hotels in Tahoe, built ugly in the early fifties but broken-in and comfortable-looking.

The woman in the office was friendly, and expressed regret that she had no vacancies. She had blue hair.

"Actually," Rosie said, "we're looking for information."

"Oh?" Polite but doubtful.

"We have reason to believe that a friend of ours stayed at this motel a week or so ago. Two friends, really, but the one we're particularly interested in finding, well... her mother is dying, and..." Nice work, Rosie, I thought.

"Oh, dear," the woman said. "And you don't know where she is?"

"That's right." I pulled out the pictures of Marjorie and Noah. She recognized them immediately.

"Yes, a really beautiful girl. Of course I remember her. She and the older man. They came in together. I remember because the man had some trouble with his car while they were here. I recommended a mechanic in town. But they only stayed a few days, and then they checked out."

"I wonder if you could tell me when they checked in and when they left. That will give me some idea..." I faltered.

"Oh, I think I could do that. I don't remember the names, though."

Since I didn't know what name Noah might have been using, I gave her the name Marjorie had given the mechanic.

She looked through her book, and found it. "Here it is. Beatrice Hinks, room 20, September 14th. Actually, she registered for both of them, late that evening."

"Registered?" Rosie asked. "With ID?"

"Well, yes. A driver's license. And she paid for both of them when she checked out. In cash.

"He'd already gone. You see, he turned in his key on"—she glanced down at the book—"Wednesday night."

"And she left when?" Rosie again.

"Thursday morning. And you know, I think there was some kind of problem, because when I told her he had turned in the key to his room, she looked upset." The woman was enjoying the drama a bit too much.

"His room?" I thought this might be an interesting point.

"Oh, yes. They had adjoining rooms. He was in 21." She leaned confidentially across the counter. "But even so, I think there might have been some kind of triangle going on there."

We waited.

"You see, not long after she learned that he had gone, another man came to see her in her room." She lowered her voice. "I heard them shouting at each other."

"Did you hear what they were shouting?" I asked.

"All I heard was the word Sonoma," she said regretfully.

"If we knew who that man was," I mused, "it would give us some idea of where she might have gone. Do you remember anything about him? He might be someone we know."

She gave us a very good description of Jerry Pincus.

"One more thing," I said. "Did the man she came here with take his car or leave it for her?"

"He took it. She asked me about rentals when I told her he was gone."

"Did she leave with the second man?" Rosie wanted to know.

"No, she didn't. I think they were angry with each other. Right after I heard them shouting, that was when I saw him. He walked across the lot, got into his car, and drove away. She left oh, maybe half an hour later. But I can't be exactly sure, of course."

"Thank you for all your help," I said.

"No trouble at all." I caught a slightly malicious gleam in her eye. "I hope you find your friend in time."

TWENTY

PINCUS WASN'T IN HIS OFFICE. I looked at my watch. Ten o'clock. But he'd said he'd be there all evening and I believed him. We got a couple of beers from the downstairs bar, bought some nickels, and sat down at a pair of slots, taking turns keeping our eyes on the door to his cubicle.

After about fifteen minutes, I was breaking even, Rosie was down a dollar, and we saw Pincus walk up to the door, unlock it, and close himself inside. We followed him.

This time I didn't knock. I just turned the knob and walked in. He looked up, startled, saw me, with Rosie an inch behind, and shook his head in disgust.

"Turn around and go right back out again, Samson." He picked up some papers and pretended to read them.

"Then I can stay?" Rosie asked.

He sighed and shook his head again. "Both of you. Out. I'm a busy man."

"We know that," I said. I sat down. Rosie sat down. I put my elbows on his desk and made myself at home. "But I'm sure you wouldn't want any trouble in your casino."

"Oh, I don't know. I wouldn't mind." But he leaned back in his chair and added, "You've got thirty seconds."

"Sorry. That's not enough. You've had a few hours since we were here before. You've had time to check on me. Isn't it funny that you still don't want to help?" It occurred to me suddenly that I hadn't been able to reach Arnold. Maybe nobody was home? But Pincus didn't bother to give me any excuses. He just shrugged and looked at his watch. I was trying to read him, trying to figure out how long he'd sit still before he called a bouncer. No luck.

"You lied to us, Pincus. You know damned well Noah was up here with Marjorie. Maybe they're still up here. You know why. I want some truth from you right now, because I'm going to find them with or without your help, but when it's all over, you're going to wish you hadn't been such a prick."

"You're an asshole, Samson. Even an animal knows when he's on someone else's territory, and knows how to act."

I stood up and leaned over his desk. "Your partner has disappeared. So has Marjorie Burns. A bunch of people back in the Bay Area think there's cause to worry, that they're in trouble. You know what's going on. They came here for a reason, and you're the only reason I know of in Tahoe. I don't think they came here to play poker or see the shows. You were seen at their motel the morning after he left, and you were having a fight with Marjorie. You want to talk to me or you want to talk to the cops?" It was a bluff and he acted like he knew it.

He stood up, too. So did Rosie. "I wouldn't give you the time of day, Samson."

"That's very original. You're one witty guy, Pincus. I just never know what you're going to come up with next."

"And you're a loser. I've known jerks like you all my life." He looked me up and down like he could see I didn't make even a paltry fifty thousand a year.

"And what have you got, Pincus? An airhead wife? A big house? Do you ever go home? Answer my fucking questions and stop playing games. You were at their motel. You know where they are. Why are you lying?"

He sat down again, his eyes very cold, a little smile on his sculptured lips. "I wouldn't bother. I told you once. I saw Marjorie. She was here on business. That's all I know, that's all I want to know. I don't give a shit what you're after or why." He pushed a button on the edge of his desk and turned back to his papers.

The man must have gotten into the casino business by winning at poker. I still couldn't read him, couldn't shake him. I wanted to punch him out, but I knew that wouldn't do any good, and besides, there was that button he'd just pushed.

I did not feel like being hustled out of his office by some punk, but the giant who showed up was no punk. He must have been six foot five and he was well armored with muscle.

"Okay," I said. "See you later, Pincus."

He laughed. "You think you'll be able to see?"

"Gee," Rosie said, when we were out on the casino floor again, "I thought you were going to push things beyond reason there for a minute. Maybe you two guys should meet on your high school football field and duke it out."

I laughed. She was right.

"Think we should stick around, see what happens?"

"I don't think so," I said. I was thinking about Pincus's threats.

Rosie smiled. "You're wondering when the goons are going to fall on us." She stopped at the bottom of the steps and surveyed the first-floor room. "I don't see any goons here."

That was when the man with the muscles slipped up behind us.

"Mr. Samson? Mr. Pincus asked me to see to it that you got to your car all right. To escort you, if necessary."

I looked up at him. He had black hair, black eyes, and very white skin, the kind that looks good in bruises. "No, thanks," I told him. "We can make it all right on our own."

"That's right," Rosie said. "I'm escorting him to his car."

The goon gazed at her blankly. "I'm not supposed to escort you, just him."

"Well, hell," Rosie said, "in that case I don't know what you're going to do." We began to walk toward the door. He stayed behind. I glanced quickly over my shoulder and caught him watching us, and, at the same time, talking into his left hand. I guess even casino bouncers have gone high-tech.

Rosie saw it, too. "I wonder why he's doing that," she said. I didn't bother to answer. When I glanced back again, he was walking about ten feet behind us. I considered grabbing Rosie's arm and running like hell for the car. I couldn't bring myself to do it. A man has to try, at least, to keep his dignity, and besides, I wasn't all that sure Rosie would agree to run with me.

So we strolled casually past the poker tables, around the chaos of the slots and out the front door.

We walked very quickly to the car, got in, and drove out of the lot.

"You know," Rosie said, "now that I think of it, Pincus wouldn't have people beaten up in his own parking lot. It would be bad for business. Can you imagine what the customers would think if they saw people getting beaten up right outside?"

"Yes. Which makes me wonder just exactly where he does plan on doing it." I was watching my rearview mirror. I couldn't tell if we were being followed. A car had pulled out of the lot a few seconds behind us but that didn't mean anything. I flipped on my right signal and cut down a side street for one block before I signaled again, turned left, and began running parallel to the main street. The car was still behind us.

"Why did you use your signals?" Rosie sounded a little scared. I know I was.

"I wasn't trying to lose them. I just wanted to know if they were following us. Now I'm trying to lose them." I turned right at the next corner—no signal—cut my lights, then left, left again for one block, right, left, and right again onto the main road.

"Lights," Rosie said.

I switched them back on. I couldn't tell whether we'd lost them or not. I'd been busy trying not to hit anything in the dark. I asked Rosie. She'd been watching out the back window.

"I'm not sure. I didn't see any lights behind us after the second right turn, but they could have picked us up again on this street. Their headlights look like a dozen other ones I can see behind us from here."

"Maybe they're just trying to scare us."

Rosie laughed. I joined her. "Let's wear them out," I suggested. "You feel up to spending a few more hours hanging around the casinos?"

"Yes."

I pulled into a huge casino lot. Again, business was brisk. People walking to and from cars. A couple of cars pulled into the lot while we were walking across to the casino's back entrance, but we couldn't be sure whether one of them contained our friends.

We went directly to the bar. Rosie ordered brandy. I was thirsty. I started with mineral water and lime.

"You know, Jake," Rosie said carefully, "if you're going to be doing a lot of this detective stuff, you might consider getting yourself a more anonymous car."

"Rosie!" I cried.

"Or at least a newer one."

I stared at her. She knows how I feel about newer cars.
At least the newer cars in anything like a reasonable price
range. No creativity, and, worst of all, no character.

The man sitting next to Rosie was staring at her hind-
quarters. He was about fifty-five, and he was wearing a
plaid sports coat, beige doubleknit pants, and brown and
white spectators. He had about half his hair. I tried not to
notice his preoccupation.

"Forget it," I told her, referring to the anonymous new
car. "If it was built after 1959 it's a clone." The man
spilled a little of his whiskey on the bar.

"This your boyfriend?" he asked Rosie.

"Yes," she said, without even looking at him. Now he
was staring at her neck. "I understand how you feel, Jake.
I don't mean to be insensitive."

"You her boyfriend?" he asked me.

"Yes," I said. "That's okay, Rosie, you're right, in a
way. But I never really plan on doing these jobs, you
know."

"Y'outta Noo Yawk?" I couldn't tell whether he was
talking to me, Rosie, or Rosie's rear end.

"No," Rosie and I said simultaneously.

Rosie continued. "Do you think they're out there waiting for us?"

"Probably not. Why bother? They can figure they've
already scared us. Maybe that's enough. On the other
hand, Pincus could be the kind of man who always keeps
his promises, especially if they're nasty ones."

"Okay. Let's go with the plan about wearing them out."
She bought some dollars, and dropped a couple of them
into the poker machine in the bar. "Want to play some
roulette?" I shook my head. "Keno?" She held onto a pair
of queens and drew another one. I realized I'd forgotten

to tell the Tuesday night group I wouldn't be playing poker with them. "Keno?" she repeated. I shook my head again. "I'm feeling lucky." She played another dollar, got four on a diamond flush and drew a spade. "Well, maybe not. Do you ever play poker up here, Jake?"

"I have once or twice, but it's too expensive. I dropped a couple hundred once, real fast, and that finished it."

"Other people lose a lot more than that, Jake, that's nothing."

"Maybe it's nothing for a rich carpenter."

"So," the man next to Rosie said. "Y'outta Noo Yawk?"

"How about some twenty-one?" I said.

On the way to the tables, I found a telephone and tried Arnold's number again. Still no answer. I thought of calling Mrs. Noah, but didn't really want to bother her. Arnold's call probably hadn't been that important.

We played twenty-one. Rosie came out twenty dollars ahead, I lost about the same amount. Over my objections, we tried roulette. Rosie was all over the place, betting on four numbers at a time. I played red. I won fifty, she lost her twenty.

We moved to the craps table. I played the pass line. She played the don't pass line. Then we switched. We both lost, and went back to twenty-one for a while.

I tried Arnold's number again at around 2 a.m. The line was busy.

By three, we were so exhausted we kept nodding off at the nickel slots.

"What do you say?" I turned to Rosie, who had dropped a nickel in her machine and forgotten to pull the handle down.

"They can't still be waiting," she said. "Let's go to bed."

But they were.

Just as we walked up to the car, two guys jumped out from behind a suitably anonymous vehicle in the next row. One of them was the giant goon. The other one was shorter but nearly as broad. The big one grabbed Rosie and pinned her arms behind her back. That was the last I saw of them before the other one was on me. I could hear Rosie yelling her head off, then a truck hit me in the stomach and I was vomiting mineral water and beer and a late-night taco all over myself. Another truck hit me in the jaw, twice. I kicked out at the truck's knees, slipped in my own vomit, and fell against a car. He hit me a couple more times until I was on the ground. Rosie was still yelling, and I could hear people running toward us, yelling back, but I couldn't quite get up. I raised my head and looked out of the eye that wasn't swelling shut. The goons were gone, and half a dozen half-drunk gamblers were trying to help me up.

"I called the cops," one of them said.

"Thanks," Rosie's voice said from somewhere. "We'll take care of it from here."

"Yeah," I said. "We're okay, now. Thanks." They were reluctant to leave us, and I hate having people watch me bleed, so Rosie helped me get in the car, took my keys, and drove us away from there.

"Are you okay?" she asked. She looked rigid with rage.

"Take it easy," I said. "I'm fine. Better than I look. How about you?"

"Nothing wrong with me," she said through gritted teeth. "That gorilla held my arms through the whole thing. I couldn't throw him or smash his instep or his shin or anything. I tried. I really tried. Nothing worked. He was huge and he read all my moves before I made them. He just held me there while his friend beat you up. After all, it wouldn't have been right to beat me up, too. I'm a woman. Goddamn sexist pigs.''

"Let's go to Jerry's Jackpot," I said. I wanted to tear the place apart.

"Are you nuts? We're going back to the motel and check you over and see if anything's broken. Then you're going to get some sleep. And so am I. We're in no shape to play any more boyish games tonight.''

I didn't argue. I felt like all my bones were broken, and I didn't smell too good, either.

I asked Rosie to give Arnold another try while I washed off some of the damage.

When I limped out of the bathroom, smelling sweeter and feeling mean, Rosie was sitting in the desk chair waiting for me.

"She's dead. Marjorie."

"Dead?"

"Murdered. Shot. Dumped on the Emeryville mud flats. Arnold's been with the cops, and with ark people, and with Mrs. Noah. It's a mess. He wants us back there right now. He says to stop wasting time out here and get back where the trouble is. I told him you were hurt and that we'd head back first thing in the morning. That we'd be there before noon."

TWENTY-ONE

ROSIE DROVE HOME. I could see okay; the eye was better. But my right knee was giving me some trouble. I'd fallen hard on it when the goon had knocked me down the night before.

We arrived home before noon, all right, stopping on the way to pick up Alice, but I decided to go to the house, first, before dashing down to the corner to soothe Arnold. I wanted to check my tape again, maybe even get my bearings.

My father was watering the geraniums.

"If I'm not here does everything die?" he said by way of greeting.

"Rico was taking care of the cats."

"I know, I know, I meant the flowers."

"How was Napa? Or Sonoma? Or wherever you were?"

"She's fine. She likes you, I think. You should call her. What's wrong with your face?"

"A couple of bruises." I continued on into the house, trying not to limp.

Eva was making lunch. "You're limping," she said. I hadn't even caught her looking at me.

"I fell."

"I told Lee you went to Lake Tahoe. I didn't tell her you went with Rosie. Sit down, have some soup. A sandwich. I bought some turkey loaf."

"I'm not hungry." My refusal was part bruised stomach, part turkey loaf.

She asked a couple of times, but she didn't push.

I limped into the bedroom to check my answering machine. No messages.

"If you're looking for messages," Eva called out, "I got a couple for you." I trekked back out to the kitchen. "Some girl named Beatrice called. Said it was important. This morning, early. Something about you should call Arnold and when are you getting home. And another one, June. You should call her."

"Thanks." I went to the bathroom, found an Ace bandage in the linen cupboard, pulled up my right pant leg and wrapped the knee. Better. I looked at my face. Blue jaw, black eye. And my stomach. Two fresh bruises, nestled in the remains of the skinning I got the night Pa got bashed.

I found the morning paper on the table in the living room and sat down on the couch to look it over. The story was on page three, at the top. East Bay woman found dead on Emeryville mud flats. There was a photo of a part of the flats, and a couple of lines under the photo that said an Oakland woman identified as Marjorie Burns, twenty-three, had been found lying partway inside the driftwood tent near the sculpture-on-a-stick of the World War I airplane.

According to the story, she had been found by a stroller the day before. A Berkeley woman walking her dog down by the Bay, on the mud flats where at least two generations of artist-citizens had created a permanent exhibit of fanciful, sometimes funny constructions that stretched for hundreds of yards along the bayfront. Permanent but organic, growing, shrinking, slowly changing as one piece falls into decay and another takes its place.

The Berkeley stroller had passed the tent, but her dog had not. The small terrier, in a classic act, had begun to whine, to approach the sculpture and back away again.

That was when the woman saw the blue running shoes, still attached to Marjorie Burns.

An execution-style murder, the paper said. Shot in the back of the head.

I had never met Marjorie, but beyond wishing that none of this had happened to her, I could certainly wish it hadn't happened that way. Execution-style. Hell, every stupid punk who can almost read knows how to do it execution-style. And then to be dumped in a sculpture in the middle of that homemade and eternal art show. And then to be found by a terrier replaying a scene from an English whodunit—well...

I decided to call June Gerhart later, hauled myself to my feet, and headed for the door. Rosie had to see this, then we'd go down to the corner. I had nearly made it out when Eva caught up with me and handed me a bowl of soup. It was green. I looked at her. "From the zucchini in your poor garden. I been watering."

"Got some work to do now," I muttered, passing my father as he came in, wiping his hands on his pants. He snorted.

"Okay, just tell us when you're running out of town again—we'll go take our trip to Lake Tahoe."

I nodded.

Rosie's door was open and I walked in. She glanced at the bowl of soup in my hand but didn't say anything. I handed her the paper, folded to the photo of the mud flats. She glanced at it, put it down again, and went to the kitchen stove, where coffee was dripping. She waved a cup at me, I said yes, and she poured for both of us. Then she sat down to read.

I decided against calling Marjorie's grandmother, considered and rejected her cousin Victor, postponed Mrs. Noah again. While Rosie read, I dialed information and got the number of the hat shop on Telegraph Avenue. Carleton wasn't at work, I was told. A friend of his had called in and said he couldn't make it that day.

I called his home number.

"Hello?" The voice didn't sound like Carleton's.

"Is Carleton Hinks there?"

"Yeah. But he don't want to talk to nobody right now."

"Tell him this is Jake Samson. Tell him I want to come over and talk to him this afternoon."

I heard the message being transmitted. The voice returned.

"He says okay, he wants to talk to you. He'll be here any time you come." I wrote down the address, and said goodbye to Carleton's friend.

Rosie had finished the news story.

"We need to go see Arnold," she said.

"Yeah. And return a call from Mrs. Noah. We also need to get hold of Hal Winter and see if he can get us anything on what the cops know." Hal is a poker buddy and a Berkeley attorney with other buddies in the Alameda County D.A.'s office.

"Speaking of cops," Rosie said, "now that they're in it, they might be visiting us."

I had thought of that, but hadn't wanted to put it in real words.

"Yeah. Anyway, we need to find out was she killed on the mud flats or brought there from somewhere else—"

"How long was she dead, what kind of gun, any other marks on the body—"

"Anything found at the scene that anyone's willing to talk about—I'll give Hal a call now."

Of course, he wasn't in. He never is. I left a message. He'd get back to me and leave whatever answers he came up with on my tape if I wasn't around. He thinks my

crimebusting efforts are funny. Which reminded me to give
a quick call to Artie Perrine, another poker buddy and the
editor at *Probe* magazine who had given me the paper that
said I was a free-lance reporter. Now that I was going to be
crossing police paths again, I wanted him to be prepared
for any queries on their part. I called *Probe*. He was out to
lunch. I left a message.

Mrs. Noah, as luck would have it, was in. She was delighted to hear from me. As a matter of fact, she sounded
delighted all the way around.

"The police are certainly interested in what I have to say
now," she said. "They're taking my husband's disappearance a lot more seriously."

"They've been to see you then?"

"I called them the minute I heard. And they took the
note he left. They went through his office, too. And they
asked me a lot of questions. About his business interests,
his friends, that kind of thing. You know."

I had to ask. "Did you tell them I took some of his
stuff?"

"Oh. No. Should I have?"

I had been holding my breath. I let it out. "No. But I'm
going to drop off what I still have. Then you can pass it on
to them, tell them you just found it. In a dresser drawer or
a closet—anywhere they haven't been. Because they would
be upset if they found out you'd neglected to give them
something." Not to mention how they'd feel about my
having it. There were a couple of those papers I still wanted
to keep; I would make copies. "Did you tell the police
anything about me at all?"

She hesitated. "Is there some reason why you're afraid
of them, Jake?"

"I'm not afraid of them," I lied. "But it's best if they
don't know I'm helping out. They might try to stop me."

"Well, I just answered their questions, and told them we had been trying to find my husband."

"Okay. You sound like you're in pretty good spirits. Doesn't it worry you that the woman your husband was with has been murdered?"

Silence. Then, "I think it's a terrible shame, of course. But they weren't together, were they? It was just her they found. And now the police will help. It's so much better with everyone trying to find him, don't you think?"

"Yeah. Better. One more thing. Do you remember the name of the cop you talked to?"

"Yes. Such a nice man. A Sergeant Hawkins."

"Ralph Hawkins?"

"I think so."

I thought about dropping the whole thing right then and there, but I'd put in too much time and blood. Hawkins and I were acquainted. I'd run into him, so to speak, when I was trying to find out who killed a local artist and tossed her off her deck. Hawkins, I was sure, had not forgotten me and Rosie.

Rosie had been listening. When I said good-bye to June Gerhart, she volunteered to run up to College Avenue and copy the papers we still had. We agreed to meet at the ark.

Arnold was working down in the hold. It was huge and dim down there, like the belly of a flat-bottomed whale, with all the ribs on the inside.

I asked him what he knew about Marjorie's murder. He didn't know much more than the *Chronicle* had printed.

"But I have this terrible fear that Noah's going to be found the same way. Somewhere. That's what I told the police, that it would all be their fault for not believing us in the first place."

"What else did you tell the police?"

"All I know is what I told you. That's what I told them."

"You didn't say anything about the fact that we've been looking for Noah and Marjorie?"

"I did mention that some of our people might have been trying to find out what happened to them, but that's all I said." He tossed me an accusing look. "It isn't as though we actually know where he is."

I blessed Arnold, in my heart, for his bureaucrat's caution.

"Is Beatrice around?"

"No. She's not feeling well today."

"Give her my condolences." I thought of Marjorie's grandmother. Condolences would never be enough, there.

"But how are you doing, anyway? Do you know anything at all? I was hoping you'd be able to keep this from happening. I certainly hope—"

"So do I. And yes, we're making headway." I told him about our visits to the Russian River and, particularly, Tahoe.

"I've always thought," he said, "that Jerry Pincus is a frightening kind of man. Cynical."

I would have used stronger words. I heard someone coming down the ladder to the hold. It was Rosie. They greeted each other, Arnold still sulky.

Rosie must have heard the tag-end of my little speech.

"We got a lot of new information, Arnold," she said. "We're getting close. We'll find Noah and bring him home safely."

Rosie's confidence shored me up, even if it was just an act. Having done her part, she began strolling around the interior of the ark and left Arnold to me.

"Yeah," I said. "And we've got a lot of work today. We'll let you know what we find out. Perk up, Arnold, you have an ark to build."

"That's right," Rosie said, ambling back toward us. "And the people up in Sonoma are ahead of you. The deck's almost finished and they have some interior plywood up..." Arnold wasn't listening.

"If something doesn't happen soon, I don't know what I'll do," he ranted. "We'll run out of money." I didn't think it was the right time to mention that I'd been on the case a week and it was time for the rate to go up to $200 a day.

"We'll talk to you later, Arnold," I said, and we got out of there, climbing up out of the belly of the beast, walking back to my car, parked in front of the house.

Our first stop was Noah's place. I left the file folders with the maid, Adele, at the door to avoid further depressed or depressing conversation. We cut back over to Oakland, Claremont to College, and from there, took Broadway toward downtown.

Carleton Hinks lived in the first-floor flat of a narrow three-story Victorian just west of downtown Oakland. I parked in a faded red zone across the street, alongside an apparently nameless warehouse or factory that showed no signs of life. I figured I could get away with it there.

Carleton's door was opened by a boy with a long, spiky crewcut and a Guardian Angels tee shirt. A young man, I guess, but I estimated his age at somewhere around eighteen.

"Jake Samson," I said. He looked at Rosie.

"Rosie Vicente," she said.

He looked back at me. "When I talked to you on the phone you didn't say nothing about two people. He don't feel so good, you know." His pale blue eyes were resentful. I was getting sick of resentment.

"I know," I told him. "But she's my partner. We're together, that's how it is." I figured that sounded enough like a bad cop show to make sense to him. It did; he shrugged and invited us in.

We let him lead us through a sunny living room furnished in wicker, bamboo, and plants. There was art on the walls, mostly posters and fruit crate illustrations, but all framed. A large braided rug seemed to float on the highly polished hardwood floor. The kid walking ahead of us was muscular, with a swagger that might have been for Rosie's benefit, might have been just self-consciousness. His chinos had a belt on the back, and he was wearing white high-top sneakers.

The bedroom was dark.

"Don't turn on the light, man," Carleton said.

I sat down on the bed next to him. "This is my partner, Rosie." He muttered hello. "I'm really sorry, Carl." He didn't answer. "I just wanted to check with you. See if the cops have been around, what they're asking about. See if you know anything about what happened to Marjorie."

He sighed deeply, with a ragged edge. "Yeah. It was the cops that told me. They said someone told them I was her boyfriend. I said I was her friend. They wanted to know when was the last time I saw her, all that shit. I told them. And I told them about the phone call, a couple of nights ago."

I stopped him. "What phone call a couple of nights ago?"

"Look, Jake, I know I should have kept you posted, but she didn't want anyone to know, she said, and I honored that. I shouldn't have. Maybe we could have—oh, shit, I don't know." His voice broke.

"What are you talking about, Carleton?"

"She called me. A couple of nights ago. Said to meet her at the flats in two hours. Would've been about eleven o'clock. So I drove on over there. I was a little late, because we were doing some planning here—you know, about that druggie that's been hitting West Berkeley—but I got there by eleven-thirty, anyway, and I sat down on that big pile of driftwood, right there where you first get down onto the flats, and I waited for her. No Marjorie. I waited until three in the morning."

"She just said to meet her? That's all she said?"

"No. She said there was big trouble. That she needed my help. I asked her what about the cops, should we bring them in on it. She said not yet. She wanted to talk to me first, figure out what to do. She sounded real nervous. Worried and scared." He stopped talking and blew his nose.

"Do you know where she was calling from?"

"No."

"Go on," Rosie urged.

"Okay, so I waited. When she didn't show up, I called Victor, and I called her grandma, and they both said they hadn't heard from her, didn't know if she was in town. Yesterday I talked to Arnold. He said he hadn't heard from her, that as far as he knew no one had, nor from Noah, either. Then last night the cops show up, tell me she's dead, start asking me a lot of questions. I told them what she said on the phone. Figured I'd better. They said they'd be back. Bet they will, too."

"Probably," I agreed. I told him how we'd picked up Marjorie's trail in Tahoe.

"She was using fake ID up there, calling herself Beatrice Hinks," Rosie said. "Do you know where she might have picked up some false identification?"

"Oh, well, there's half a dozen guys around her neighborhood. Easiest thing in the world. It might not be good, might not get past a cop or a bartender, but it would be okay for most purposes."

"Tell me this," Rosie said. "How long would it take to get hold of a fake driver's license? If you knew who to go to? Hours? Days?"

"Same day."

"You wouldn't have any idea who she might go to for that?"

"Nah. Like I said, could be anybody."

Even so, the information was helpful. It meant she could have found out she needed to cover her movements, gotten fake ID, and taken off for Tahoe all in the same day.

"Have you talked to her grandmother since she was found?"

"Yeah. I called over there. She's pretty bad. Got a neighbor in to look after her. Victor did, I mean. She wasn't talking to anybody."

"Do you have any idea why she might have wanted to meet you at the mud flats?"

"It just kind of worked out that way. See, she seemed like she was afraid to go home, and she said she didn't want to meet anyplace that, well, she might be watched. I don't know what she meant. I guess whoever killed her.... Anyway, we used to go there, together, sometimes. It's real peaceful. So we just agreed to meet there."

I stood up, reached over and squeezed his hard shoulder, and told him to try to get some rest. The crewcut kid met us in the living room and escorted us to the door.

I took the parking ticket off my windshield and stuck it in my pocket.

Naturally. It went along with everything else. We'd started out with a nice, cozy little disappearance the cops couldn't have cared less about. Now some vicious son of a bitch had gone and complicated things. I had to come up with some way of telling what I knew to the cops—withholding evidence in a homicide is not something the law looks upon kindly—without admitting that I'd been investigating the case. The old magazine writer cover would have to do it. Or maybe Arnold.... I needed to think it through a little.

But the only thing my brain would focus on was that someone I was supposed to be finding was dead.

TWENTY-TWO

EMERYVILLE IS A CITY, a weird little waterfront append-
age stuck onto the Bayside of Oakland. A mishmash of
houses, restaurants, warehouses, businesses, condos, tall
corporate headquarters, and low-ball poker clubs. And
the Emeryville mud flats.

As far as I know, there are only three ways to get down
to the mud flats. You can pull up on the shoulder of the
freeway and climb the cyclone fence, you can take a boat
in until it scrapes bottom and wade the rest of the way on
foot, or you can approach from Powell Street. From
there, it's a short hike across the flats to the sculptures, a
pleasant enough challenge if you're wearing waders,
which we were not.

I parked in the Holiday Inn lot and we crossed Powell. The highway department's ice plant at the roadside,
which squashes unpleasantly underfoot, gave way almost immediately to wild grasses, which gave way again
to a muddy bank dropping down to the flats. We half
picked our way and half slid down the bank, sloshing
over to the biggest collection of driftwood, the warehouse of raw materials, a deep cut full of tons of wood,
huge planks and poles, smaller bits crisscrossed in the
mud, all interspersed with odd bits of metal and trash and
big chunks of styrofoam from God knows what or where.
It was here that Carleton had sat and waited for Marjorie.

Rosie led the way across the bridge of flotsam. A
sandpiper screamed, nearly upsetting my balance. An-

other one took up the call. Standing on a perfectly beautiful two-by-twelve that I knew I could find some use for around the house, I turned to watch the birds. There were three sandpipers running around on the shore yelling at me, and when I slipped off my plank and fell against a charred telephone pole, a flock of doves I hadn't even seen, those small beige doves you see everywhere in the East Bay, took off. Oddly, there were no gulls. Gulls circle the parking lot of my neighborhood Safeway, miles from the Bay. Gulls hang around downtown Berkeley. But here, on the Bay itself, I didn't see even one.

I turned back in the direction of the sculptures. Rosie was waiting silently for me, twenty feet ahead, on a hillock of grass.

"Birdwatching," I said. She nodded and negotiated a tricky leap from the hillock to a cross-hatch of railroad ties three feet away, sliding dangerously on their muddy surface, catching herself, and stretching a leg toward another patch of semidry grass. I, passing lightly, Nijinsky-like, over the last of the dry footing of nearly solid driftwood, reached a stretch of mud and water-logged turf, following Rosie's trail along the slightly dryer, upper side of the flats nearer the freeway fence.

Rosie had already entered the field of art, so to speak. The sculptures were still some distance away from me, stretching to the south. I stopped again to get my bearings, to look toward the exhibit, when I saw a flashing movement, just to my left. A pale orange cat, small, wiry, was watching me from its perch on yet another chunk of phone pole—is there a country in the South Pacific where a revolution against ITT has been launched? Was the cat lost? More probably abandoned, maybe as a kitten. Probably wild. A survivor, admirable and smart. I called to it.

"Hey, cat, don't be scared. Want to come home with me? Here kitty..." I was sure Tigris and Euphrates would understand and accept a poor refugee. The cat continued to stare at me. Afraid, interested, maybe even wishing it could believe me, but too frightened to approach. Face to face at twenty feet but no closer. I turned my head away for an instant, to find Rosie. When I turned back it had vanished into the brush.

Rosie was standing under a huge humanoid figure, waiting, again, for me to catch up. I nodded to her, held up my hand, took a deep breath of the unnameable soup of undefinable ingredients, and sloshed on, trying to find solid footholds, failing half the time.

The driftwood art of the Emeryville mud flats tends to the abstract. I hadn't really looked at it lately. A quick glance from the freeway every so often. Lots of human-like figures and some animals. Looking around me, straining my eyes in the mist-glare of the afternoon, I thought I remembered that there had once been more representational art out there: more real-looking objects and machines. But maybe some of today's abstractions were the ruins of those earlier creations. It could have been ten years since I thought I saw them.

The closest one to me was a human, or a tyrannosaur, or something, nine feet tall. A post with assorted scrap propping and climbing it. A mane of aluminum fringe. A big styrofoam head, mouth open, red tongue sticking out. A single protrusion—a unicorn horn?—sticking out of the middle of its head.

There was a gallowslike structure with a piece of wire fencing hanging, executed, from it; a horse-shape, maybe fifteen feet at the head, and another big horse, farther on, to which Rosie had now progressed. To the left, a thing with two wheels that looked vaguely like a dive-bombing airplane.

A windmill.

A cross complete with shreds of martyr.

Rosie had reached the one we were looking for, the first one that offered a shelter for a corpse. Tent-shaped, plywood propped against car tires and two-by-fours. Alongside it, a picket fence, or six pickets of one, that seemed to go with the little tent in a casual way, was stuck upright in the mud.

To get to Rosie, to get to the tent, I was going to have to cross some very wet land, and go a dozen feet closer to the Bay than the track I was following. I didn't expect to find anything there. My shoes were already soaked. I stepped off the plank from which I'd been surveying the art show, down onto soggy grass. Up to the laces of my white running shoes.

The water was six inches deep in spots; some of those spots had planks laid across them, bridges for sculptors. I used the planks when they were there to use, but mostly I slogged. Through sticky mud that damned near sucked my shoes off; through drowned grass.

I passed a door, propped by two-by-fours, upright, looking closed for some reason. A boat shape perched on a pillar of phone pole. I ran out of bridges and sank shin-deep, negotiated the other foot around to higher ground, did a couple of hops and a jump, and reached Rosie and the tent.

"Anything?"

Rosie shrugged. "Looks like someone's been here. But then," she added, "someone has."

Lots of someones. The mud was churned to the consistency of cheese spread, a distasteful item even on crackers, where it's supposed to be. Squatting as best I could in the mush, I looked inside the little tomb. The surface was gouged by the pushing and pulling of a body, and by the feet of laboring cops. A few footprints disappearing into the marsh grasses. Nothing interesting stuck in the mud or the sculpture, or at least not any more. No bits of clothing, hanks of hair, bloodstains. No crouching killer.

I got down on my knees and crawled inside. Not much doubt that the structure had been there a long time. Rot was creeping up its deeply mired sides. I pulled out my pocket flash and checked more carefully. Crud. And enough room for two if two should want to have a cold and sloppy alfresco screw. But like Marjorie's had, someone's feet would have stuck out. I exited backwards.

"You're a mess," Rosie told me.

I stood up.

"Think she was killed here?" Rosie asked.

"I guess. Followed. Killed. Shoved inside. To hide the body? From Carleton?"

"Maybe just to delay discovery. How would they know she was meeting someone?"

I nodded. "He didn't see anything or anyone. He just sat there and waited, he says." I glanced to my left, toward the cyclone fence and the freeway, the southbound traffic no more than a hundred feet away. The top of the fence, in a direct line from the wooden tent, was bowed out of shape. But that could have happened in 1973. I pointed it out to Rosie.

"Who knows?" she said. "Marjorie would have come over from Powell, like we did. The killer could have followed her from there..."

"Not without being noticed, coming down the bank."

"Right. She'd run."

"And he'd chase her down. Maybe he shot her while she ran, got her in the back of the head."

"Hard to do, isn't it?"

I agreed. I thought about it. "What if there were two of them? One of them went down the bank, the other one drove the car along here, hopped the fence, and caught her running from the other one. Neat. Then they tied her up, shot her and stuffed her in the tent. A shot, out here, with all the noise from the freeway?"

"Sure," Rosie agreed morosely. "That would work great. One shot. A few screams. No trying to hit a moving target in the dark in the mud."

"Or Carleton met her, killed her, stuck her away."

"Or the killer got off a lucky shot and dragged the body out here to hide it."

I turned to the right. A dancing human figure, twelve feet tall, of rusted scrap. Beyond that, the Bay, the Bay Bridge, The City and its conglomerate skyline of old and new San Francisco. A little farther to the north, the Golden Gate and Marin, the Marin headlands hiding in the afternoon fog.

"I wish she'd been killed somewhere else," I said.

"Why?"

"Oh, hell, I don't know. But if I thought I was going to die, it would break my heart to know I was looking at that"—and I waved my arm at the view—"for the last time."

"You're a romantic son of a bitch, Samson."

"I know."

We stuck around for a few minutes, just thinking about it, then hiked back across the marsh to the Holiday Inn. We took our shoes off and banged them around for a while, trying to get rid of some of the mud. Then I pulled an old blanket out of the trunk and spread it on the front seat to protect the Chevy.

Inside the closed car again, the stink of swamp on our shoes and clothing was nearly overwhelming.

"I wonder how it really happened," I said.

Rosie sighed. "Academic. She's dead. She knew something and someone killed her. Or someone killed her because they hated her."

"Or because they loved her."

"Horse shit."

"It happens."

"Not in this case," Rosie said. "It's all got to do with whatever made Noah and Marjorie run off in the first place."

"There's something else I don't get," I said, maneuvering the car out of the parking lot. "Why would anyone walk a dog in the mud?"

On our way back to the house, I stopped at a liquor store and picked up an afternoon *Examiner* and an *Oakland Tribune*. The *Examiner* had a tiny blurb on the murder, the *Tribune* had a slightly bigger one that solved, at least, one of the small mysteries. It included a paragraph about the woman who'd found the body. She and her dog went down to the mud flats frequently, she said, because "there's a cat living there. We're trying to adopt the cat."

TWENTY-THREE

THERE WAS NO MESSAGE from Hal on my machine, but that would have been a little quick, anyway. He might not have anything for a day or two.

Eva was in the kitchen cooking. Pa, she said, was taking a walk with his friend Rico. She invited Rosie for dinner, but Rosie said she had a date.

"Such busy people," Eva clucked, mixing just the right amount of regret with her joy at Rosie's social success.

Dinner would be ready, I was informed, in an hour and a half. Rosie's date was not for two hours, so we went to the cottage to take care of a chore that was best, I thought, done quickly.

I had considered going to Ralph Hawkins and laying it all out for him, telling him everything I'd learned about the case so far. He was a very sharp cop, a very good one, and the point of this whole thing, after all, was to return Noah safely to the bosom of his cult. We were no longer playing hide-and-seek.

There was a problem with that approach. I wanted very badly to stay on this case, and once Hawkins told me to butt out, I would be on very soggy ground, even as an "investigative reporter" for *Probe*.

Best if the cops didn't know we were in it at all. Rosie and I talked about it. She agreed. What we would do, we decided, was write out everything we knew, every word we remembered, every lead, every physical clue, take the story to Arnold and tell him to give it to Hawkins. Arnold would say that this was all the information culled by all the ark people who had been trying to find Noah and Marjorie.

We started at the beginning and worked our way through, with me taking notes.

"Here's how it looks," Rosie said, handing me a glass of orange juice. She was out of beer. "Noah leaves a note saying he's got something to do, and he and Marjorie take off for Tahoe. That's the start, right?"

"I don't think so. Marjorie went somewhere early Saturday morning. We don't know whether she came back or not, but sometime during that day she picked up some false ID. Then she and Noah took off. With the ID and with the quarter of a million."

"He wrote a check for the money, but there was no payee listed in the check register and the check has never been paid in."

"Right. And just a few days before he disappeared he told Arnold to speed up the construction. Why would he do that and take off with the money?"

"Maybe," Rosie mused, "he never did take off with it. Maybe he gave the check to Arnold before he went, saying, 'Here, finish it off fast,' and Arnold has it stashed somewhere."

"Interesting point. Maybe Arnold's been stashing a few dollars here and there all along."

"Which could explain why the Oakland ark is not as far along as the one in Sonoma. They've started some finishing work up there on the walls—bulkheads?—but not here. He could be cutting some corners, biding his time." She poured us more orange juice.

"Possible. But why would he hire someone to find Noah?"

"He didn't think he had a choice, with Beatrice recommending you as an investigator and Mrs. Noah pushing for some kind of action."

I drank another half-glass of juice, which was beginning to give me a heartburn. "All right. Let's leave it at that. Either Arnold's got the money, which I doubt, or Noah and Marjorie took off for Tahoe with it. Why take the money to Tahoe?"

"The man is crazy. Maybe he had a dream or got a message that he could quadruple his stake at the craps table."

I laughed. "Makes as much sense as anything else."

"They were in Tahoe for several days. Then Noah takes off, Pincus shows up at the motel and has some kind of fight with Marjorie. Over the money? Someone says something about Sonoma, and Marjorie takes off."

"Yeah, but what's Pincus got to do with Sonoma?"

She shrugged. "Unknown. Then, a few days after Marjorie leaves Tahoe, she calls Carleton. She's scared, she wants him to meet her. And she winds up dead. And still no sign of Noah and no word."

I scribbled a few more lines on my notepaper. "Got any pretzels?" She pulled a bag out of the cupboard and dumped it into a bowl. They were stale, but I ate one anyway. "Meanwhile, let's not forget that someone sent a punk to scare me off, and the dumb shit clubs my old man."

"That's the kind of thing Pincus seems to enjoy. Scaring you, I mean."

"But the guys in Tahoe were not the guys I saw here."

"I'm sure Pincus has lots of employees."

I ate another pretzel. "About Arnold—he seems so dedicated to the arks. Real nervous about running out of money, about getting them finished."

"If he took the money, he'd be nervous."

"If he never got the money he'd be nervous."

Rosie took a pretzel, bit into it. "These are stale."

"Yeah. What have we forgotten?"

We ran through the notes for a few minutes.

"That Saturday they took off," I said. "Marjorie left home early in the morning, Noah left home somewhere before early afternoon, Marjorie called her grandmother in the evening, they checked in late that night at Tahoe. None of it seems to fit very tightly."

"Neither does Noah's head," Rose said uncharitably.

"True. I think we've got everything here. Sonoma seems to be the last lead from Marjorie, before she came back here. I want to go back up there. And on the way, why don't we stop at Yellow Brick Farms. I'd like you to check it out with me, and I want to find out what the cops have said to Durell and vice versa. And meanwhile, I guess I'd better give Lee a call."

"Was that too casual? Did I hear a tone of voice that was a little too casual?"

"I don't know what you mean."

She snorted at me. I handed her the bowl of stale pretzels. She said since I was going to be so busy calling Lee, she would take our summary over to Arnold, along with the request to pass it on to Hawkins. As the product of many minds.

I wished Rosie a happy dinner, told her I'd talk to her first thing in the morning, and trotted back to my house. Pa was back from his walk. Dinner was still fifteen minutes away. I went into my erstwhile bedroom and closed the door.

Lee answered on the third ring. She sounded glad to hear from me. We chatted about Pa and Eva, and what a good time they were having.

Then I said, "I'm going to be up in Sonoma tomorrow. If you're free in the evening, maybe we could go out for a drink or a movie or something."

She was free. We decided on dinner and a movie she'd heard good things about. I wrote down her address, on F Street near downtown Petaluma. Of course, almost everything in Petaluma is near downtown Petaluma.

I would see her at six.

Eva was setting the table when I came out of the bedroom. Tonight was fish, she said. Poached salmon with green beans, beets, and parsley potatoes.

"A light meal," she said, "because none of us is getting any younger."

My appetite thus dulled, I sat down to eat.

"So, big shot, your face is healing pretty good. Been chasing muggers again?"

"No, Pa."

"He was brave that night when the man hit you," Eva objected. "You shouldn't pick on him."

"Pick on him? Who picks? But you know what they say about brave?"

"No," I replied. "I do not know what they say about brave." The fish was good. My appetite was returning.

"Neither do I, but curiosity killed a cat."

"And a stitch in time saves nine."

"And," Eva snapped, "you should both grow like onions with your heads in the ground."

The old Jewish curse shut us up.

The phone rang just as I was bringing out the coffee.

"Hi, Jake. Playing Batman again?" It was Hal.

"No. Captain Marvel. Shazam. What's up?"

"We missed you at poker. It's at your house next week."

"I'll have to call you."

"Okay. Now about this Marjorie Burns—you know she was a Guardian Angel?" I told him I knew.

"She was shot with a .38, back of the head, hands tied behind her back, all that good shit. And it happened there, on the flats. There was, as they say, a struggle, because she was mud all over, and it looked like she did some running before they caught her—prints and stuff, hard to pick out in that mess, but enough."

"Any hints about the alleged perpetrators?"

"You're right to make it plural. There was a witness—a passing motorist. Not a real good witness, because he was zipping by on the road, but he saw a car parked on the shoulder and he saw a couple of guys climbing over the fence from the flats, real fast, jumping into the car. He thought it was pretty strange, so he didn't forget, and when he saw the story in the paper about Marjorie Burns, he called the cops."

"Anything on the guys or the car?"

"The car was a dark-colored, older model, big. And one of the guys, he said, was blond. Some of you white folks really stand out in the dark."

"Yeah," I said, "but sometimes people can't tell us apart." I told him about the punk who'd come looking for me and gotten my father. "So, if the cops make the connection between that police report and this homicide, I'm tied in in about forty ways."

"Maybe I don't know you. Maybe we should plan on having the poker game somewhere else. Like the Oaks club."

"I've had enough of Emeryville for a while."

"That's all I've got. Except you know she disappeared with some guy a couple of weeks ago?"

"Yes."

"They're looking for him."

"Isn't everybody."

"Oh, and there was the thing about her identification. She had two IDs, her real one and a phony in the name of Hinks. They found her rented car on the Holiday Inn lot. Rented as Hinks. That's all I got." I thanked him for his help. "No problem. But you'll have to tell me all about it when I've got more time. See you Tuesday, I hope."

I took my coffee out on the front steps. Eva went into the bedroom to watch *Wheel of Fortune*, and Pa joined me.

"Eva wants to go to Lake Tahoe," he said. "We thought we'd take one of those buses, go up tomorrow, stay a couple of days, come back, stay here a couple days, go home."

"Sounds like fun," I said absently.

"I never gambled, except a little pool in the old days, a little cards for pennies. What's a good game?"

"There's Keno. And craps. And twenty-one. And of course the machines."

"Ah. The one-armed bandits."

"Yes, those."

"What is this twenty-one?"

So I showed them, when Eva's program was over. We played for a couple of hours. I was the house, and I won.

TWENTY-FOUR

THE FIRST THING I did the next morning was go down to the cottage and call Victor's junkyard.

"What do you want, Samson?" He sounded more tired than unfriendly.

"I wanted to tell you I'm sorry about Marjorie. To ask how her grandmother's holding up. And to ask you if you remember anything now you didn't remember the last time I talked to you."

"Okay. Yeah. Right. Sorry. Look, I'm not feeling too good. Her grandma's feeling worse. And I don't remember anything at all. What is it you want me to remember?"

"About Sonoma. You said you remembered she told you she was going to Sonoma. It would help a lot if you remembered when she said she was going."

"I been thinking about that. I can't be sure. But you know, I kind of have this feeling it was late in the week she told me. See, my wife doesn't remember her dropping by, and my wife she generally takes off on Friday."

"And you still don't remember her saying anything about Tahoe?"

"No. She sure didn't say anything about Tahoe."

"Okay, thanks. If you should think of anything, please give me a call. Meanwhile, take it easy, and give my best to her grandmother."

"Thanks, man. Life sure is a piece of shit sometimes, ain't it?"

"Sometimes, Victor."

I told Rosie what he'd said. "Sounds to me like that's where she went Saturday morning." I drank a cup of Rosie's good coffee and told her about my date that night.

"So it's Yellow Brick Farms, then north to the ark, then you head back down to Petaluma," she said. "I'll follow you up in my truck for the working part of it. Unless you want me along on your date."

"I don't think so. Take your truck."

Durell was in, but the woman at the front desk told me he was busy. This was not Doreen, Durell's Saturday secretary, but a much younger woman who seemed unbearably bored. If we could wait half an hour or so, she said, he would see us. We said we could. We went outside to stand in the sun. It wouldn't be many weeks, now, before the rains started again.

"This place looks big," Rosie commented. "Let's walk around."

There wasn't anything else to do, so we walked. When we got around to the back, just beyond the loading dock, I noticed some broken glass on the ground. Looking at the wall above it, I saw that the window had been newly replaced—bright white glazing putty, shiny new glass. Rosie was peering into a dumpster near the dock. I called her over.

"Boost me up," she said.

A second later, I heard her say, "Oh, hello." The window shot up and Durell stuck his head out. Rosie dropped to the ground.

"Samson! The receptionist told me you were here. Why is your friend peeking in my window?" He was startled, and not amused at all.

"It's a lab," Rosie told me.

"Sorry, Joe," I said. "I wasn't planning on peeking in any windows until I saw this one had been broken."

He shook his head, still not amused. "Come on back around to the front, both of you. I can talk to you now."

His office door was open and he waved his hand at the side chairs.

"What happened to your lab?" Rosie wanted to know.

He smiled grimly. "Burglar. I guess we'll have to put up some bars."

"What did they steal?" I asked.

"I don't know yet."

"Looks like they did some damage," Rosie said. "That wasn't just window glass you were cleaning up."

"Burglars are clumsy. Maybe it was some druggie looking for something. There's plenty of ex-flower children up here, and half of them are crazy."

I was remembering something. Something I'd read in Noah's papers. "Wasn't there an employee? Someone you fired? He was complaining to Noah, saying you had no reason to let him go. Wasn't he connected with the lab in some way?"

"I don't know who that would be. It's a good-sized company, sometimes we have to let people go."

"This was pretty recently. And he was connected with the lab."

"That's right," Rosie said. "I remember it, too. Howard. William Howard."

Durell snapped his fingers. "By God, that's right. He was my lab assistant. Incompetent, unfortunately. He took it hard." He thought a minute, and shook his head. "But if you mean he did the burglary—out of spite or something—he wasn't that kind of man."

"Have you got an address or phone number for him?"

He sighed and pushed a button on his intercom. "Annie? Would you see if you can find a personnel file on

William Howard? Terminated.'' He thanked her and turned back to us.

"Now, Samson, what did you come up here to talk to me about? I heard about Marjorie, by the way. That's a real shame.''

"Yes, it is. I suppose the police have been here to talk to you?''

"Sure have. They wanted to check out his office. I think they also wanted me to tell them that Noah killed her, but I couldn't exactly do that. They asked me if I knew anything about the two of them going to Tahoe. Say, I think you must know the cop I talked to.''

"Why do you say that?''

"When I mentioned your name he acted like it was familiar to him.''

Wonderful. I didn't think I'd call to check my answering machine while I was away from home. There might be something on it.

Durell caught my look. "Maybe you didn't want your name brought into it? Hey, I'm sorry Jake. All I said was that you'd been doing some checking around, looking for Tom. Nothing wrong with that, is there? This is a murder case, after all.''

I didn't say I'd already noticed that. "There's something else, Joe. Arnold says that just a few days before Noah took off he told him to speed up the work on the arks, that the flood was coming sooner than he'd first thought. Know anything about that?''

"Only that I heard that's what he said. That everything had to move faster. Kind of makes you wonder, doesn't it? To say that and then to take away the money. Just doesn't make sense. Well, if that's all you need, I've got one hell of a lot of work to do.'' He pushed the intercom button again. "Annie? Did you find that file? Good. Pull out the

address and phone number and give them to Mr. Samson
He's on his way out."

Annie handed me a slip of paper as we passed her desk
Howard's address was in Glen Ellen. Annie gave us directions.

Number 517 was a duplex. Neither of the names on the
bells was Howard. I rang the bell for the downstairs flat.

The elderly woman who answered the door smiled
warmly at us, but said Mr. Howard no longer rented her
upstairs.

"You were his landlady?" Rosie asked. "When did he
leave?"

"Yes, this is my house. He left, oh, it's been nearly a
month ago, now. I was sorry to see him go. Are you friends
of his?"

I nodded. "Do you know why he left?"

"Well, I'm afraid it was because he lost his job, poor
man. He was working nearby, you know."

"Yes, I know. Do you have a forwarding address for
him?"

"I certainly do. Let me just go find it." She was gone for
just a few seconds. "Here you are, you can write it down.
He said he was going back home because nothing made
any sense out here, those were his words."

I looked down at the slip of paper. William Howard
had, apparently, gone back to Cleveland, Ohio.

"Do you know that he went right back east when he left
here?"

"Oh, yes. I got a postcard from him . . . oh, three weeks
ago it's been. From Cleveland."

Not wanting her to think I wasn't grateful, I copied the
Cleveland address into my notebook.

TWENTY-FIVE

PASSING THROUGH GUERNEVILLE, I honked my horn at Rosie, who was leading the way. She pulled over; I pulled up behind her and aimed an index finger across the street toward the restaurant with the award-winning pancakes. It was lunchtime, and I don't like to work on an empty stomach.

The place was crowded, but we found a booth.

"I noticed," Rosie said, "that you didn't tell Durell we were coming up here."

A slice of tomato, greased with mayonnaise, slid out of my hamburger with the first bite. I managed to drop it on my plate instead of my lap. "I don't want anyone to be expecting us. I didn't want our questions stage-managed this time."

She nodded thoughtfully. "We never did hear what any of those people actually said to Fred, did we?"

"No. And it doesn't make sense that no one would remember what day she was here—especially if she did come early that Saturday morning. Some of the ark crew must have weekday jobs, some must come only on nights or weekends. There must be some difference between the days up there. And it would have been early. Someone has to have noticed."

"And if someone did notice, and no one's telling us..."

"Yeah."

We ran through several hypothetical time-lines, disappearance through murder. We picked at the bits and pieces that were beginning to come together in what looked like

a sketchy but logical trail of leads. Sketchy because there
were big chunks that didn't seem to fit at all, that had to
be stuck over to one side for a while.

Fortified with food and scenarios, we crossed the street
again and got into the cab of Rosie's pickup, an oven after an hour parked on the sunny street. Rosie dug a red
sweatband out of her dash compartment and pulled it over
her dark hair. She had just started the engine when I saw
a familiar-looking car cruising by. A big old American car,
early seventies, dark blue. A dent in the passenger side
door. I caught a glimpse of the rear license plate, just
enough to read the first three letters: CYC. I couldn't see
if the driver had blond hair, and there was no passenger.

I told Rosie. She shot the truck into gear and took off
after the blue car. We were one curve behind, but the dust
hadn't settled on the dirt road to the ark. We held our distance the rest of the way. By the time we got there, the blue
car—it was a Pontiac—was parked off to the side of the
clearing next to another car that looked familiar—a white
Toyota. We pulled in behind, blocking the way out for
both of them, and went looking for Fred. Yellow-haired
Fred.

He was up on the deck with the owner of the white Toyota. Doreen, the Saturday secretary at Yellow Brick
Farms. We climbed the ladder.

"Whose car is that?" I pointed at the Pontiac.

"The Toyota? Mine. Why?" Doreen asked.

"The Pontiac."

Fred took over. "It's just an old car we use around here
for errands. Everyone uses it."

"Who just drove it in here?"

"I did," Fred answered.

"You use it for a lot of errands, don't you?"

"What are you talking about?" He laughed.

"This is Doreen," I told Rosie. "She works at Yellow Brick Farms on Saturdays." I turned to Doreen. "You up here a lot?"

"I help out."

"Do you ever help out on Saturdays?"

"How could I?" she asked reasonably. "You just said I work at—"

"Right. I'd like to talk to someone who does work here on Saturdays. Excuse me." I saw a pair of workers down at the far end of the deck and walked toward them. Rosie headed for the hatch.

"Excuse me," I heard Fred yell, "but where do you think you're going?"

I turned to look at him. He was talking to Rosie, who was poised at the entrance to the hold.

"I just want to talk to whoever's down there," she said.

"No one's down there. And this is private property. And neither one of you should be bothering our workers. They're busy."

"So are we," I answered. "And we're here to ask some questions."

"Fine. Talk to whoever you want. Just don't keep them from their work. But there's no one below."

Rosie didn't argue. She nodded agreeably, crossed the deck, and climbed down the ladder to the ground.

I started with the two I'd spotted earlier, up on the deck. One of them was tossing plywood scraps down to the ground. Neither one of them had ever met anyone named Marjorie, and didn't remember seeing anyone who looked like her.

Doreen and Fred were still standing on deck, watching me. I waved at them and climbed down the ladder, looking for Rosie. She was nowhere around. One by one, doggedly, I picked off the rest of the crew, and got pretty much the same answer from all of them. Nobody knew what I was talking about.

Fred came down to stand next to me, looking impatient, while I talked to the last of the workers. When Rosie appeared suddenly, at the edge of the clearing, pushing her way through the ferns, he noticed her emergence, frowned, but said nothing. She wasn't wearing her red sweatband any more.

"If you two are finished..." Fred sighed.

"Tell me something," Rosie interjected conversationally, "Do you bring your supplies in by road?"

"Well, of course. What else would we do?"

"I was just wondering. You must be pretty close to the river on this side." She jerked a thumb back toward the woods she'd just come out of.

He laughed, a superior chuckle. "You couldn't move serious building materials or anything down that river. It's too shallow and too slow, especially this time of year. And why would you even try? You can pull a truck right in here."

Rosie shrugged. "Just wondering. Change of pace, maybe."

He shook his head, tolerant but weary. "We're not playing games here, you know."

"I'm sure you're not. Well, thanks for your help."

We got back in the truck. She swung it around and drove slowly back along the dirt road.

"What was all that stuff about supplies?"

"Just fishing," she laughed.

"River talk," I parried.

"No, really. I was wondering what they use the river for. There's a canoe tied up on the bank back there. The river's only about three hundred feet away from the ark."

"Will we be able to find it?"

"Yes."

I looked at my watch. Two o'clock. "Let's go rent a canoe."

We went back to the same motel we'd stayed in a few days before.

"Here again?" the clerk asked, pen poised over the registration form.

"Not to stay," I told him. At least I hoped not. I had a date in four hours.

We set off downstream, paddling hard. It didn't take very long to go the distance, not much longer than by car.

"There it is," Rosie said quietly. I looked over at the river bank, to our right, and saw the canoe, half-hidden in bush. But Rosie was pointing up, above the canoe, at the marker she'd left wrapped around the branch of a bay tree, well above eye level. Her red sweatband.

We pulled our own boat aground a dozen feet from the other one, just out of sight behind an eroded bank.

Rosie climbed the tree to retrieve her sweatband and stuck it in her pocket. A dozen feet from the water, we were into deep woods. Bay, shrubbery, oak and poison oak, with the redwoods towering just ahead.

We couldn't have been far from the ark, if Rosie's estimate of its distance from the river was anything like accurate, but I didn't hear anything. No hammering. No sawing. I was wishing they'd make some noise so I wouldn't have to move so damned carefully. There were dry twigs everywhere, and between maneuvering around nature's noisemakers and the prolific poison oak—bright red and easy to spot, anyway—I was so alert I quivered.

I heard something. I grabbed Rosie's hand and dropped behind a fallen bay tree.

"Probably a deer," she whispered.

The deer, which had not seen us, stepped out from behind a redwood tree on two legs, carrying a heavy-looking canvas bag, dressed in filthy camouflage pants, shirt, and cap. His face was smeared with mud. The beard was longer than in the photo I had, and the frizzy hair stuck out from under the cap. Noah. Rosie pinched my hand, hard, so I knew she recognized him, too.

I froze, torn between wanting to watch him secretly and wanting to grab him and cart him home before anyone got in any more trouble.

Rosie, however, never freezes. Which is good and bad.

"Psst! Noah!" She wrenched her hand out of mine and stepped out from behind the tree. His eyes widened in his dirty face, and he turned into a deer again, bounding out of sight.

We went after him, but he could have been hiding anywhere in the brush. "Well, hell, at least we know where he is. Or was," I added bitterly.

Rosie shushed me with a wave of her hand. "He's all right. The important thing now is the ark." We crept on, following the trail she had left to the clearing: broken branches, little piles of needles and cones. "You know, I'll bet that was his canoe." I guessed so.

We were getting close to the ark, she said, but there were still no sounds of work. Dead quiet. Except for a sudden soft rustle to our right. This time I wasn't going to take any chances. I hurled myself at the source of the sound. He rose up from the ferns like a mountain, and that's what he felt like when I crashed into him. The goon from Tahoe. The big one. He clamped a hand over my mouth, but Rosie hit him with a flying tackle and he fell back into the undergrowth again, grunting, pulling me down with him. Rosie had found a branch the size of a baseball bat. She swung at his head. I tumbled out of the way. She was stopped in mid-swing by the goon's partner, who leaped out from behind a tree and grabbed her arm. Same partner as before, the one who had mashed me in the Tahoe parking lot.

We all smelled the smoke at once, and we froze like four grown-ups playing that old kids' game, Statues. Goon number one, sprawled facing me, mouth open, head turned toward the ark, still hidden by the trees. Rosie, frozen with raised branch, forearm in the grip of Goon number two. I, squatting on the forest floor, head raised, nose wiggling like a rabbit's.

Smoke. And the crackle of fire. All the statues came alive, racing for the clearing.

I smelled gasoline and saw the can lying on the ground near the ark.

Noah was running toward us, scuttling like a crab, looking back at the fire that had eaten half the ladder and was blackening the hull. I grabbed him. His canvas bag was empty. Fred came over the rail, started down, jumped the last eight feet to the ground, stumbled, recovered, and headed for me. Doreen was standing on the deck waving her arms and yelling. Another man, who hadn't been around when I'd talked to the crew members before, climbed down the scaffolding—the ladder was now gone—carrying an ax. He ran to the burning section of hull and began hacking at it. Something about his run, his sneakers, his size: it was the punk who had mistaken Pa for me that night at the house.

Tahoe Goon number one intercepted Fred. I was still holding Noah, who was laughing his head off.

None of the other ark workers was anywhere in sight; the two cars were gone from the clearing. A Corvette pulled in to take their place. Joe Durell leaped out, ran to the ark, and looked wildly around for the ladder. He

started to run toward the guy with the ax, saw me clutching Noah, and pulled a gun. Goon number two pulled out
his own gun and shot Durell in the shoulder. Durell's
weapon dropped to the ground and so did he, screaming.
Doreen stuck her head out of one of the holes the ax-
wielder had made and yelled, "Is the fire out?"

The axman yelled something back, but none of us heard
it. The soft rhythmic percussion I'd barely registered, a
background beat for the scene on the ground, swelled to an
ear-battering racket as the helicopter appeared above the
tall shivering trees and hovered over the clearing, beating
the smoke down again in suffocating gray waves that
pushed me and my laughing prisoner back to the edge of
the woods.

Doreen reappeared at the hole in the hull and began
tossing dozens of little plastic bags full of white stuff out
to the guy with the ax, who dropped his firefighting
equipment, grabbed an armload of bags, and ran for the
Corvette. Which could no longer be maneuvered out of the
clearing because the Sonoma County Sheriff's car had just
pulled up tight against it.

And out of the police car, along with two shotgun-toting
deputies, came a couple of men in street clothes. One of
them was Sergeant Ralph Hawkins of the Oakland Police
Department.

In the distance, I heard sirens.

TWENTY-SIX

THE COPS WERE ROUNDING us all up when the fire truck
bulled its way down the road. The helicopter had backed
off, and the smoke was clearing.

The firefighters checked out the ark, chopped a few
more holes in it, and said something into their radio. The
helicopter clattered off into the distance.

Hawkins was saying something to me about "free-lance
writers really getting around," but I was watching another cop who had crawled into the ark through a door-
sized hole. He took over where Doreen had left off,
dumping out armloads of plastic bags. Another cop, with
a much bigger bag, was collecting them.

I didn't get much of a chance to watch, though. More
cops had arrived and we were all hustled down to the
sheriff's office for questioning. Hawkins separated me and
Rosie, but I figured she'd know how to handle her end of
things.

Hawkins concentrated on me.

Yes, I told him, we were helping our neighbors at the
Oakland ark look for their lost leader, because I was hoping to get a story of some kind. After all, a bunch of crazies building an ark? Great copy. He sneered at me.

Yes, I admitted, Rosie and I had picked up the trail of
Noah and Marjorie in Tahoe. Yes, we'd seen the papers.
We knew she had been killed. No, I had not gotten the
message he'd left on my answering machine that afternoon and I didn't know he wanted me to call him. That
was true.

Then I really started lying. Putting on my best innocent-idiot face, I asked why we would think it was strange that Durell had fired his lab assistant and had a different secretary on Saturdays than he did the rest of the week.

I also said it had never occurred to me that Durell might be using the ark for a drug warehouse, even though yes, of course, we knew he was a chemist. Had we seen the insides of both arks? Yes. Then we must have noticed the plywood sheathing on the walls of this one. Of course. Rosie was, after all, a carpenter. But why, I protested, would we think it was strange that no one was putting up any plywood in Oakland?

As a matter of fact, we'd been slower on that than we should have been. We'd seen Noah's construction sketches, along with his other papers, early on. But they were Noah's, and we didn't take them seriously. Until more pieces fell into place, we just assumed they were incomplete.

Hawkins let me make a phone call. I called my lawyer, but only to tell her I would probably not make it for our date that night and would call her again when I was free.

After yet another hour of questions, they put Rosie and me in a room together. We compared notes carefully, on the chance that the light fixtures might have ears. While we were talking casually about what we had said we didn't know, they opened the door and another wrung-out specimen stumbled in. Jerry Pincus.

A small but adequate adrenaline rush propelled me toward him. He held up his hands and said, "I'm sorry, Samson."

"Yeah?" I snarled, grabbing the front of his shirt.

He didn't seem to notice. "Yeah. I tried to call Arnold that night to check you out, but I couldn't get an answer. I didn't know who the hell you were. For all I knew, you were out to get Noah and Marjorie.'' He glanced up at the ceiling light and raised his voice. "Of course, I called the police the minute I heard about Marjorie, to tell them what I knew."

That left a lot unexplained, but the Jerry, who represented a piece of the picture we hadn't been able to fit in yet, wasn't about to talk any more that day. Not to me and not in that room.

Hawkins turned us loose in the small hours of the morning, promising that he would see us the next day in Oakland and we'd better keep ourselves available if we knew what was good for us.

Over the next three days, we each got a few more sessions down at Oakland Homicide, and putting those sessions together with what we learned from Noah and from Jerry Pincus, we managed to fill it all in.

During my last visit with Hawkins, on Sunday, he had told me he was anxious to see the story I wrote for *Probe*. "You be sure and send me a copy of it," he said.

Pa and Eva came back from Tahoe Monday morning.

"I saw the papers up there," Pa said, when he thought Eva was out of earshot in the yard. "Big dope raid on an ark. Wasn't this ark. Was another one. Theirs, too?"

"Yes, Pa."

He nodded slowly, heavily. "Rico and me, we thought there was something fishy. That Arnold, very fishy. We knew there must be something wrong over there."

"It wasn't Arnold, Pa."

"It wasn't Arnold that what?" Eva demanded, marching in the front door. "It was a dope fiend that hit your father, yes?"

"Not exactly, Eva. Well, yes. A dope fiend. Sure."

"We're leaving tomorrow," Pa announced. "No more dope fiends. Next time you come to visit us. Now, let's you and me go say hello to your tenant." He was going to insist on an explanation.

Eva would be neither distracted nor fooled. "We'll all go down, you'll tell us what's what. You think I can't read newspapers? You think maybe I didn't notice something a little funny, you with a black eye, dope fiends in the yard?"

So we all went down to the cottage and Rosie and I told them what was what.

The part that took the most explaining was the part about the designer drugs. Pa remembered reading the story in the paper about the fake heroin that was flooding the market and turning people into vegetables.

"It was the same thing?"

"No. Something new. Not even an imitation of another drug. Brand new and not illegal—because nobody's made it illegal yet."

"So how could the police arrest them?"

We decided to start at the beginning.

Durell had to be aware that other people, many of them chemists, were making fortunes by mixing their own drugs. All it took was a few quarts of ordinary chemicals and a little know-how, and you had a fortune in street dope. Millions of dollars worth of untested—but who cared about that?—drugs.

Durell had access to the chemicals. He had a lot of know-how. And he had a laboratory. Unfortunately, he owned only a small share of the business, about a quarter of a million dollars worth, and his partner was around a lot.

Then Noah had his vision. He started building his arks. He didn't have time for Yellow Brick Farms anymore. Durell was pretty much on his own. As long as he kept the business going, no one, not Noah and certainly not Mrs. Noah, would interfere.

All he had to do was get rid of his hard-working, conscientious lab assistant, who would certainly be able to tell that the lab was being used on weekends no matter how carefully Durell cleaned up after himself. Get rid of him and bring in a part-time employee to help with packaging and deliveries. Doreen. The Saturday secretary.

He checked out the drug laws and found the loopholes. There are the illegal drugs and there are the ones that aren't illegal yet.

Under state law, an illegal drug like heroin or cocaine is illegal whether it is, according to the California Supreme Court, "produced directly or indirectly by extraction from substances of vegetable origin, or independently by means of chemical synthesis."

"That means," Rosie interjected, "that if you imitate an illegal drug—the one the court was ruling on there was imitation cocaine—you've still got a banned drug."

Eva looked blank. Pa was squinting painfully. "But if you come up with something brand new," I added, "the law can't convict you. The new stuff you make—call it jellybean-x—has to be outlawed before it's illegal to make and sell." Their eyes cleared somewhat.

So Durell came up with something new. Nothing crude, and no mere imitation. It didn't melt people's brains, but the high made them feel powerful, confident, Godlike. You get the wrong people feeling like that, you've got mean. Like the guy who was battering old folks down in West Berkeley so he could stay up all the time.

Durell had managed to get only one batch on the street before he was stopped, but its effects were going to be felt for a while.

That first batch was the one Marjorie saw being delivered to the ark early one Saturday morning.

Because Marjorie, growing up as she did, where she did,
had a suspicious mind, and it kicked in when Noah told
her they had to push the schedule up because Joe Durell
had had a dream of prophecy. He had dreamed, Noah
said, that the flood was coming in December, a month
sooner than they'd thought. They had to hurry. Durell
himself would spend more time at Sonoma, pushing the
project.

Marjorie didn't like or trust Durell and she didn't for a
minute believe he'd had a vision. She figured he had another reason for hanging around the Sonoma ark, for
wanting it built faster.

She went up to Sonoma, early in the morning on the
14th, earlier even than the crew was due to arrive. She left
her car parked down the main road and hiked in. Durell,
she saw, had been busy down in the hold. A finished
bulkhead, sheathed in plywood, a refinement that wasn't
in the plans. She fiddled with it and it slid open. Empty.
She heard a car coming, climbed up out of the hold and
down the ladder to the ground, and hid in the woods. She
saw the Toyota pull in. Doreen and Joe Durell got out,
opened the trunk and started unloading boxes. Doreen
dropped one. A couple of plastic bags fell out. When
they'd gone, Marjorie drove like hell back to Oakland to
tell Noah.

Noah, I explained to the folks, refused to call the police. Against Marjorie's protests, he called Yellow Brick
Farms. Durell was there. Noah told him what he knew and
said he was on his way up to talk to him. He didn't want
to go to the police, he told Durell. He didn't want his
project destroyed, his good works ruined, his cult blown
away by scandal. He begged and he threatened and he of

fered a deal. He would buy Durell out of the business, buy him off.

Durell told him to come right along to Yellow Brick Farms and they would talk about it.

Noah took a check from his book, registering the amount he planned to write, and wrote a note to his wife. Yes, he admitted to Marjorie, he was worried about what might happen at the plant, but he had to go.

Marjorie drove his car, and she took him, not to Sonoma county, but to someone she knew of in West Oakland who made false identification. Sure, she hated criminals, but she was desperate enough to buy the services of one. She knew they had to get away and that they had to cover their trail. She couldn't force Noah to call the police, and she didn't want to go against his wishes by calling them herself, but she had another plan, and during the hours while they waited for the fake paper, she convinced him to go along with her.

They drove to Tahoe. She didn't want to get her Guardian Angel pals involved in a drug situation, but there was someone else who might be willing to help: Jerry Pincus. If he couldn't talk Noah into calling the law he could at least try to keep him away from Durell. And, she figured, they'd be safe with Pincus.

"Wait a minute, wait a minute," Pa interrupted me. "Why should this Durell be so worried? You said his drug is not illegal?"

"Even so," I said, "he could be arrested and he could be stopped. See, it works like this: the cops see you sneaking around with a lot of plastic bags full of white powder, they've got what they call 'probable cause' to arrest you. They take the stuff to a lab for analysis. Meanwhile, you're out on bail, with the law looking over your shoulder. They're going to go ahead with the prosecution while they

try to figure out what they've got in those bags. If it'
something really new and it's not a banned substance
you'll get off. But by the time the whole mess is over anc
you're free, the machinery is in motion to make you
jellybean-x illegal, and the cops know who you are. You
could try making something else, but . . ."

"But meanwhile, a business worth tens of millions o
dollars is out the window," Rosie concluded. "And that'
why Durell was so worried."

"And that's why Marjorie, who was planning to disap
pear with Noah, was so scared," I said.

So they went to Jerry Pincus, who was horrified. Noal
tried to talk Pincus into going to Sonoma with him. N
soap. Pincus said he would try to protect them, somehow
but if they didn't call the cops he would. Noah begged fo
some time to think it over, and Pincus agreed, reluctantly

Noah kept after Pincus, but he couldn't break hin
down. He gave up and decided to go to Sonoma himself
even though he hadn't decided what he would do there. H
was, by now, convinced that Durell might be dangerous.

When Marjorie discovered he was gone, she called Pin
cus, who went to the motel. She blamed him for not doin
a better job of keeping Noah safe. She said she was afrai
he'd gone to Sonoma.

Pincus still wouldn't agree to help. He fought witl
Marjorie about calling the police, but agreed not to do i
himself, less, I suspect, out of loyalty than out of a grow
ing unwillingness to get involved in the mess.

Marjorie went after Noah herself. She holed up with
friend in Santa Rosa and drove to the River every day
looking for him, asking at motels, scared to death th
whole time that someone from the ark would spot her. Th
Santa Rosa friend, who called the police when Marjori

urned up dead, said Marjorie seemed terrified but wouldn't tell her why.

Actually, she needn't have been so worried at the River. Durell was busy at Yellow Brick Farms that weekend, giving me my virgin tour of the plant, and then, with me safely gone, getting to work on the second batch of jellybean-x. Once he'd met me, he decided to dispatch Fred and friend to the Bay Area to knock me around a bit and scare me off. And have yet another try at picking up the fugitives' trail.

They were still in the East Bay a couple of days later when Marjorie, unable to find Noah, went back to get some help from her friends. But Fred got to her before Carleton did.

Noah, meanwhile, was camping out in the woods, meditating. While he was asking for divine guidance, he had enough sense to keep his recognizable car hidden on a back road. He made his decision. He stopped in Guerneville to pick up a can of gasoline and get something to eat, saw the paper, saw what had happened to Marjorie. He went wild. He drove to Yellow Brick Farms. The lab door had a new lock on it. He went out back, broke in, and tore the place apart. Then he went back to the Russian River, rented a canoe and paddled to the ark, hiding in the woods, waiting for his chance to finish making the world clean again. Not a flood this time. Fire.

Pincus had by then also heard of Marjorie's death, called the police with a half-story, and, he said, feeling somehow responsible for Marjorie, sent his own men to the River to try to find Noah.

Durell, reasoning correctly that Rosie and I had found his trashed lab mildly suspicious, sent Doreen to the ark to warn Fred that we were in Sonoma and might be headed up that way. They told the crew we were criminals, and if

we showed up asking questions they should tell us noth
ing.

When we showed up, they stashed Fred's partner in the
hold, afraid we might recognize him from that night in
Oakland. After we left, they sent the rest of the crew
home. Durell was on his way; they were going to move the
white stuff out.

Then we all had our picnic in the woods.

Durell would get off on the drug charge. Jellybean-x
would be outlawed, but the ban wouldn't be retroactive.
He would not, however, get off on the murder charge.
Fred's passenger in the old blue Pontiac, the big guy who'd
bashed Pa and helped to kill Marjorie, was babbling and
plea-bargaining like crazy.

"They should throw away the key," my father said.

"And you, you should be locked up, Mr. Jake Sam
son," Eva railed at me. "You're crazy. Don't you ever do
anything like this again!"

"I won't," I lied. Pa looked at the ceiling for help from
God, but he didn't get any.

Eva stood up. She knew what to do in a crisis. "I'm
going to make dinner, now." She glared at Rosie. "You
come, too."

After dinner that night, I called Artie Perrine, my pal at
Probe, and told him they had to run something on the
story. He said Chloe would call me and they'd come up
with something I could show to Hawkins. A piece on de
signer drugs, maybe.

Then I called Lee. Since I hadn't heard from Hawkins
for a solid twenty-four hours, I figured I could make plans
to go to Petaluma without having to worry about cancel
ing them.

"You're sure you'll be able to make it tomorrow,
Jake?" she asked.

"Positive."

"I remember you saying something about being an investigator of some kind?"

"Yes. Sort of."

"There was a really big drug bust on the River that night."

"I know."

"Will you have an interesting story to tell me?"

I laughed. "Yes."

"Good."

TWENTY-SEVEN

I TOOK THE FOLKS to the airport the next afternoon. Ric
wanted to come along for the ride to see his new buddy off
and I warned Pa in advance not to say a word to the ol
man. I didn't want him strolling around the neighbo
hood telling stories about me.

"Undercover, right?" Pa said.

"Yes."

He sighed. "Well, I guess it's better than being a bum.

On the way back home, Rico said, "It was that Arnol
wasn't it? He hit your father over the head."

"No. It wasn't Arnold."

"You should watch him. I don't trust him. You keep a
eye on him, okay, Jake?"

I told him I would.

I stopped back at the house to feed the cats before I wen
on to Petaluma.

No luggage anywhere. Nobody cooking or yelling at
newspaper. Rosie wasn't home, either. I sat in my livin
room until I couldn't stand the solitude any more, and the
I headed north.

I got to Petaluma early, drove around for a while, an
pulled up in front of Lee's house on F street promptly
six.

She looked gorgeous. She was wearing a soft gree
blouse that matched her eyes, and very tight pants. W
went out to dinner, and we went to see that movie she'
been wanting to see.

It was a pretty stupid movie. I don't remember much about it. Something about spies, and some jerk who gets mixed up with them. I've never understood the fascination with spies. They seem like a pretty tacky bunch to me.

We shared a box of popcorn, no butter, and we held salty, but at least not greasy, hands.

She also thought the movie was stupid. "That's the last time I'll ever take George's recommendation," she said, as we left the theater with the small crowd. We walked to a nearby bar for a nightcap, a trendy place full of trendy people.

"Who's George?" I asked, after I ordered a Czechoslovakian pilsner.

"I think I'll try that, too," she told the waiter. "George is someone I work with."

I wanted to ask more about him, but that wouldn't have been too subtle.

She liked the Czechoslovakian beer.

"You were going to tell me why you missed our date the other night," she reminded me.

Since I planned to keep seeing this woman I came clean, told her all about it, told her about the other times I'd done this kind of thing before.

"Designer drugs," she mused. "Tricky, very tricky. You know, there's a California congressman who's introducing legislation about that. He wants to go beyond banning the drug itself, beyond banning its imitations. He wants to make it illegal to produce and sell a drug that has the same effect as any illegal one."

I hadn't known that. She was wonderful. She knew everything.

"But couldn't someone come up with something that had a whole different effect?"

She shook her head. "I don't know. I suppose. But there are only so many effects that people want a drug to have, and we've probably managed to cover most of those already."

"Might work," I agreed. "But I worry about laws that are too general."

"So do I. They usually don't work very well." We ordered another beer. She was watching me, smiling. "Speaking of legal problems, aren't you playing a very tricky game yourself?"

I smiled back at her. "Yeah. I am. But these things come along every so often, and Rosie and I have gotten to like the challenge. Or the excitement. No, I think it's the challenge."

"What happened to the arks? What happened to Noah?"

"He's okay. He's blaming himself for Marjorie's death, says he should have called the police. The police agree, and he's going to have to work that out with them. Meanwhile, Mrs. Noah is trying to put Yellow Brick Farms back together. And the arks—Arnold's back to the old schedule, and things are quieter in the neighborhood at night."

"What happened to Jerry Pincus?"

"Noah covered for him, said he didn't know about the dope."

"I hate to sound like a lawyer," Lee said, "but why don't you get a license?"

"I've thought about it. I could get one, I guess. I don't know. If I had a license I'd have to follow the rules. I've gotten used to not having anyone looking over my shoulder."

She laughed. "A genuine free spirit." Right. But I was beginning to have a problem with that. I'd been thinking that I liked Ralph Hawkins. That I didn't like lying.

Someone else could have gotten hurt if he hadn't been fast enough, and sharp enough, to show up when he did. And maybe what I hated most of all was having to act like a moron in front of him.

Lee interrupted my musings. "This Rosie," she said. "Tell me more about her." I told her.

It was a weeknight, and she had to go to work the next morning, so I took her home around midnight. She offered me coffee "for the road." I drank the coffee. I kissed her.

"Thank you," she said.

"For the kiss?"

"No. For not saying it's a long drive back to Oakland."

"It is." I kissed her again. She kissed me back, but she moved away.

"Haven't you been reading the papers?" she asked.

"Yes. What—"

"The old free days are gone. They're saying this is the age of restraint."

It was a long drive back to Oakland, but we had a date for the weekend.

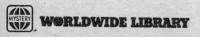

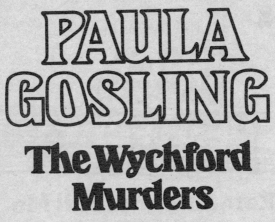

Can you keep a secret?

You can keep this one plus 2 free novels.